GRAY DAWN

HAILEY EDWARDS

Edited by Sasha Knight
Copy Edited by Kimberly Cannon
Proofread by Lillie's Literary Services
Cover by Damonza
Illustration by NextJenCo

GRAY DAWN

Black Hat Bureau, Book 10

In this tenth and final installment of The Black Hat Bureau series, Rue races the clock to find her little moth girl before it's too late. As much as she wants to believe that Clay will protect Colby, he isn't himself when he's under the director's thrall. And the director would toss a loinnir back like a shot of pure magic if he got his hands on her.

As if Rue doesn't already have enough heaped on her plate, Luca is spreading her poison west in a twisted game of take-out roulette. Now Rue must decide if saving one life is worth sacrificing the dozens of innocents Luca will kill if Rue doesn't make stopping her the top priority.

As the director, Rue ought to put her agents' lives and the Bureau's purpose above her own, but Colby is her child and—right or wrong—Rue would burn down the world to save her.

CHAPTER ONE

Twenty-one hours left until Calixta expected me to deliver the director in exchange for reducing Aedan's sentence from a lifetime spent in her court as a slave to her whims, to ten years in service as her heir. Four hours ago, I would have been ecstatic to learn Calixta hadn't picked apart my threadbare plan to liberate my cousin. But three hours ago, my short-lived triumph came unraveled as my heart was ripped from my chest and stomped into pulp on the glittering sand before the mocking sea devoured it in lapping waves.

Clay had betrayed me.

He hadn't meant to, hadn't wanted to, hadn't had a choice, but he had done it all the same.

And when he disappeared with the director, my only leverage with Calixta, he had taken Colby with him.

Hold on, my little moth girl. Be brave and strong as only you can. I'm coming for you.

The steady beat of my heart was proof she was still alive, but for how long was anyone's guess.

The director had been in a bad way before the fight that blew the roof off his cabin in Lake Okeechobee.

If he drained a *loinnir*, it would restore him to perfect health.

1

If he drained *Colby*, it would kill her and me both.

The only thing keeping her alive, I knew down to my marrow, was the golem who wouldn't recall why he had a moth in his pocket. A child he couldn't protect if his master discovered her and ordered him to...

"The Kellies."

The leather strap of the quartz pendant I had been dowsing with above a sun-faded paper map slid from my fingers to thump onto the card table. I had been hunched over it for a solid hour, willing the stone to show me the path to Colby through our familiar bond. I could have thrown a dart and had better luck.

Without magic, the tether between us was a dead end. I couldn't rely on it to locate her. I had to find another way.

"Hmm?" I blinked away the state lines superimposed on the backs of my eyelids. "Oh. Isiforos. Hey."

Saltwater dripped from his hair, and his eyes were bloodshot. Shivers wracked him, chattering his teeth.

A thread of tension had strung taut between us since the moment he let Clay walk out with the director. I couldn't blame him for recognizing Clay's authority, but we had yet to pinpoint who put the director on the phone with Clay. Whoever facilitated the exchange had allowed the director to seize control of Clay.

The missing guard, who never returned from his lunch break, was my guess. Just another loyalist I would be plucking out of the Bureau's ranks like weeds for years to come. But the urge to cast blame or wallow in guilt made things awkward between Isiforos and me. I regretted it, but I didn't know how to fix it.

"You didn't wear a wetsuit?" I grabbed a towel and draped it across his shoulders. "Are you insane?"

As soon as he realized what he had done, what he had cost me, he drove to ground zero from where the director had been hidden. He parked his SUV, walked past my tent, unable to meet my eyes. He rode the lift down, walked into the ocean to join the divers collecting debris, and I hadn't seen him since.

"The Kellies." He smacked the map with his damp palms and sent the table wobbling. "I found them."

Most of the missing had been recovered from the sea, so it had only been a matter of time. "Good."

"No. Not good. Fucking *great*." He jabbed a dripping finger in my face. "They're alive, Rue. *Alive*."

"Alive?" I couldn't wrap my head around the concept of good news. "Arthur Kelly and Kelly Angelo?"

With their help, we could get the Bureau back on its feet. We could organize the agents and assign cases instead of letting them sit on their hands until I figured out how to coordinate efforts between agencies, packs, covens, etc., and our myriad outposts. We could get back to work.

"I've never actually met them." His excitement fractured in the face of my reluctant belief. "I didn't have the clearance for it." His gaze slid to the dirt at my feet. "Those are the names they gave." He raked a hand through his hair, scooping it away from his face. "A vampire and a gargoyle."

As much as I wanted to believe the tides were shifting in our favor, I wasn't ready to trust our luck yet.

"Start at the beginning." I needed a second to process what this could mean for us. "Tell me everything."

"I doubled the size of the team when we switched our focus from rescue to salvage. The extra hands let us work faster to clear the rubble, so our newest team was dispatched to a new quadrant a few hours ago." They must have hit the water on Isiforos's orders the second Calixta and her retinue exited the area. "Their team leader informed me they heard rhythmic tapping from within the rock. The team listened until one of his guys determined it was Morse code. Once he heard the pattern a few times, he was able to decipher it. The same message was repeated after a ten-minute interval."

As I grasped for something real, I found the leather cord in my hand. "What was the message?"

"'Send blood. Tired of old-ass vampire biting me. Also livers. Chicken. Cow. Human. Not picky.'"

3

"That…sounds like something Kelly would say."

Thirty years into their service, the Kellies had slipped their leashes, fled to a small town in Pennsylvania, and slaughtered a human family in their beds. Arthur drained each one down until he was too gorged to flee the scene then climbed in bed with a corpse and waited for the agents to collect him. Kelly hadn't fared much better. She glutted on organs, crawled out the front door, and passed out like a drunk on the lawn where the dawn turned her to stone.

Neither of them had been allowed to leave the compound, for any reason, since.

Until now.

"Medics are with them." Isiforos stood in a puddle of his own making. "Where do you want them after they've been cleared for duty?"

"Boston." I swallowed past the lump rising in my throat. "Clay has a decent setup there."

The thrill of building a new database from scratch had made Colby giddy.

So had the black card I entrusted to her sans parental controls.

"Rue…"

"I don't hold what happened against you." I had trouble shaping the words. "It wasn't your fault."

It was mine.

For allowing the others to forget Clay wasn't always a friend. That he wasn't always safe. But I loved him too much to ostracize him during the stretches when he was free to be himself. His authentic self. It gutted me to erase the person they knew so I could draw them a clearer picture of who he was when his autonomy was stripped away to expose the shell controlled by his current master.

The real question was—how had the director gotten Clay on the phone? Who let him place that call?

We had to track down the missing agent, but he was just one item on a to-do list that stretched to infinity and beyond.

"Agree to disagree." He stepped back. "I'll begin preparations to contain the Kellies at The Spinnaker."

"Send our best witches ahead to secure a ballroom for their use. Ward it top to bottom. Keep fresh guards in rotation in case the Kellies get any ideas about reliving Pennsylvania." I entrusted him with a kernel of rare knowledge. "The Kellies are magically bound together. They can't get more than fifty feet from one another. If they escape, they'll go together. That makes them easier to track." I clenched my fingers until the cord bit into my skin. "Keep them happy. They can order whatever they need to get our operation up and running. They can request foods or drinks, but nothing with a pulse. Actually..." I bit the inside of my cheek until it stung. "Maybe email me their requests, and I'll approve them myself until you get the hang of it."

"Okay. Yeah. Sure." He lingered in the entrance of the tent. "I'll do that."

The pruned fingers of his right hand toyed with the ties on the canvas tent flap. He sucked in a lungful of air, parted his lips, then left without another word as Arden joined me, raising her eyebrows at the map.

"I'm new to the whole magic thing, but are those splotches where we should search or Isiforos's tears?"

"Too soon," I chided when I couldn't find the humor in our circumstances.

"Sorry." Using the hem of her tee, she blotted the soggy paper. "No luck?"

"None." I glowered at my palms, willing the skin to tingle with power, begging my fingers to prickle with an uncast spell. "I have no magic." I choked on a laugh that made my ribs ache. "I can't even dowse."

Humans armed with forked sticks and a prayer for water were more accurate than my pendulum swings.

Annoyed with myself, with the whole situation, I dropped the quartz and stomped it into the sandy soil.

"You have magic." She pocketed the trash then gathered my hands. "You just can't access it right now."

"What good am I to anyone like this?" I searched her face. "I'm basically—"

"—human," she finished for me without bitterness. "You were human when I met you."

"Technically," I interrupted, "I have always been a witch."

"For argument's sake, we're calling you human for the duration of this pep talk since you lived like one."

"Noted." I squared my shoulders. "Carry on."

"You were human when you launched Hollis Apothecary out of your home, when you hired Camber and me, and when you gave us real jobs with actual responsibilities. You never treated us like we were dumb kids. Or food. Or playthings. Or spell ingredients. You treated us as your equals."

"And when you two suggested I open a storefront…" I saw where this was heading, "…I listened to you."

"Exactly." She dug her nails into my hands. "So, listen to me now." She stared into my eyes, right down to my soul. "You're not worthless without magic. You're not powerless without magic." She risked a hesitant smile. "You're still you. Still Rue. Still my mentor and…my friend."

Tears stung the backs of my eyes as I reeled her in for the bone-crushing hug I had been wanting to give her since she first stepped off the plane. "Thanks." I sniffled against her cheek. "I'm glad you're here."

A cool wind tore at the tent flap, and Asa walked in dressed in white from head to toe. His hair had been braided into intricate loops accentuated by the rainbow flash of an opalescent hoop piercing his septum. The small studs in his ears glinted with a metal I couldn't identify. Even his hair sparkled with glitter.

"I see you're back from the land of Faerie." Arden pinched her lips together, but a snorting laugh choked her. "I've watched all of *The Lord of the Rings* movies, but they didn't prepare me for this."

"I've been in meetings with my grandmother and a visiting scholar priest in The Holy Temple of Divine Reflection for days," he explained away the flowy tunic and loose pants. "This is standard attire required for the children of priestesses while the council is in session."

As the son of Priestess Callula and the grandson of High Priestess Naeema, he must have gotten a double whammy in the stylist's chair to make him this shimmery.

"*Days?*" Arden gawked at him. "You were only gone three hours."

"Three hours here," I said to her on my way to him, "is about forty-eight hours there."

"Are you serious?" A slow-building wonder brimmed in her eyes. "That's *so* cool."

As soon as my cheek hit his chest, I breathed in the green-apple scent of him and felt the caged animal in me quit its frantic pacing. A hint of sweet cherry tobacco laced his skin, and knowing Blay was home too let me breathe for the first time since he stepped through the portal Dad anchored for him near the spot where Blay had burned the otdrel corpses to ash.

"Did your grandmother, or the scholar priest, have any good news for us?"

"He believes the only way to remove the Hunk is to behead you, but he also expressed concerns that the Hunk would grow stronger for bathing in your blood. There is also some concern it would view your death as a sacrifice made in its honor and become more sentient." His slow exhale rustled my hair. "As much as I enjoyed visiting with Grandmother, the trip was a waste of time we don't have."

We hadn't tried decapitation as a method of Hunk removal, true, but it wasn't like it would sit idly by while I let the ax fall. Though, now that I thought about it, we hadn't tried any potentially lethal methods since I got cut off from my magic. Who was to say, with it bound within me, that it could act even to save itself?

"We had to try." I kissed the underside of his jaw. "We'll just have to find our own solution."

Dad had promised to work on one, and since he was one of the authors of the Maudit Grimoire, he had a better shot of breaking its hold over me than High Priestess Naeema. The Tinkkit choker she created for me had been twisted by black magic, which was Dad's specialty.

"I heard Isiforos found the Kellies." He tightened his hold. "They really carved out their own safe room?"

"They did indeed, which proves they knew the compound was rigged with explosives."

"And they had enough warning," he agreed, "to hide before the compound came down on their heads."

Arden scratched her forearm, wincing when the scab flaked off and a perfect crimson drop formed over what was fast becoming a scar from her constant picking. With Colby gone, and my magic off the table, I would have to fall back on my white witch ways. A salve was just what the doctor ordered to soothe her irritated skin.

Comfrey and plantain leaf, lavender, and tea tree essential oils, with extra virgin olive oil and vitamin E.

That should do it.

Really, since this was Arden, who had worked at Hollis Apothecary for years, I should give her the recipe.

"I'm going to find Fergal." She caught me frowning at her and hid her arm. "He has a job for me."

Once she was out of hearing range, Asa angled toward me. "You should warn her about the Kellies."

The last thing we needed was for her to get it in her head that because Fergal was approachable that the Kellies were too. "I plan on it. I'm debating how much she needs to know. Their history is messy."

The old setup made fraternization next to impossible. It kept their interactions with other agents to a minimum. This new arrangement presented challenges, among them allowing for social-ization that the Kellies might use to finagle their way out of confinement.

"Arden should know they're two of the most prolific killers the Bureau has ever enlisted."

"There are a *lot* of things Arden should know and twice as many she shouldn't but..."

"You'll tell her if she asks."

"If she asks, yes. I will." I drew in air between my teeth. "I don't want to lose her again."

"I don't think there's any chance of that." Amusement softened his features. "She's glued to Fergal."

I made a noncommittal noise in the back of my throat and strode out under the moonlight for fresh air. "The Kellies could make the difference between Black Hat catching its balance or falling flat on its face."

"Their recovery makes a great many things possible, but it doesn't solve the problem of Aedan."

"No." I hated to admit how stuck I was on that point. "It doesn't solve Aedan."

"We need to buy time with Calixta while we locate and secure the director."

"I'm open to suggestions."

"She's a new queen, and her position is precarious. She won the throne through a fair challenge, no one can contest that, but it's clear she holds the Haelian Seas kingdom in higher regard than Hael."

"That sounds an awful lot like you're saying we should lean into the civil unrest."

"Thanks to Carver, we know there's a movement to put me on the throne." He wiped glitter from under his eye. "Stirring the pot is dangerous, but we have several advantages. The centuria being the largest of them. They know how to make an impact, without blood-shed, and they can contain the situation. And, if it comes down to it, I can offer to appear in Hael and give my endorsement of Calixta."

Aside from that last part, which was *never* going to happen, I had to agree it was a solid plan. But eager as I was to shout *let's do it* from the rooftops, I still had to ask him, "Are you sure about this?"

Asa might have given up his title, but he wanted the best for his former kingdom, and this was not it.

"We need a distraction. If we convince Calixta her crown is in peril, she will refuse to leave Hael. She'll contact us and ask for an extension, which gives us the time we need to locate the director."

"I asked you once if you're sure. I'm not a good enough person to ask you twice."

"I wouldn't have offered if I wasn't convinced this is our best course of action." He kissed my fingers. "I'll contact Moran and organize our efforts through her."

"What do we tell her?" A groan tore out of me. "About Clay?"

"Nothing," Asa decided after sitting with the question. "We keep his absence quiet for now."

Moran would take her boyfriendlike person—they hadn't stuck a label on it yet—having his switch flipped about as well as I was taking Colby's disappearance. But she would accept the news with a stiff upper lip if it came from Asa. She still viewed him as her liege, even though Aedan had claimed his title.

From me? Clay's best friend? The person who should have kept him safe?

She wouldn't be half as deferential or as forgiving of my failure.

"All right." Coward that I was, I relaxed into his decision. "I'll text Carver, let him tag along. He has the inside track, so we might as well put him to use."

>*I've got a mission for you.*

>>*I'm all ears, my lady.*

>*Moran is heading into Hael. I want you to go with her. She'll give you your marching orders there.*

>>*Should you need me, you only have to send word, and I will return to your side.*

>*I'll do that.*

A commotion near the lift drew my attention to the arrival of the helicopter we kept on retainer. A black metal box with finger-sized holes in its sides used for transporting dangerous creatures from urban areas swung from chains under its belly. A flatbed would arrive soon to haul the Kellies to Boston.

A throat cleared behind us, and I turned as Fergal stepped forward with his lips pulled tight over his teeth.

"Let me guess." I felt the universe cock its fist and take aim. "We have a problem."

CHAPTER TWO

"Your father has returned." Fergal turned his gaze skyward. "With help."

A ball of limbs spiked with struggling wings grew silhouetted against the moon, and I squinted to see if Dad was carrying Mom. Except Mom tended to curl against his chest, not chicken dance across the sky.

"I wasn't the only one dispatched, I see." Asa twitched his lips. "Maybe Saint had more luck than I did."

Except I hadn't issued orders to either of them. I hadn't been in my right mind. I wasn't sure I was now either. Asa had decided to make one last appeal to his grandmother, in the hopes she had figured out a way to remove the Hunk so that I could get my magic back.

With my magic restored, I could trace Colby through our familiar bond, find her, and bring her home.

Without that connection, I wasn't sure how to locate her hidden within the spells the director cast to cover their tracks.

Dad had left shortly after Asa. Without a word to me. Not one I registered anyway. Numbness had seeped in by that point. I was used to him appearing and disappearing, so I hadn't questioned him about his plans.

Clearly, that had been a mistake.

"Is that…?" I jerked my head toward Fergal. "He flew in a warg?"

A long howl in the distance told me a second one wasn't far behind, and my heart beat in my throat.

"Yes." He smoothed his tie. "From the looks of it, she didn't appreciate it much."

"She?" I wiped a hand through the air to erase the inane question. "I know who it is."

From the amusement bright in Asa's eyes, he had identified our incoming guests too.

Before I could determine Dad's drop zone, a lean gray beast exploded from the hill with a snarl. "Derry?"

The wolf ignored me and began leaping, higher and higher, attempting to clamp on to Dad's leg and drag him to the ground. A beat later, flames erupted out of the corner of my eye as Blay emerged with a grin.

"Derry friend," he called, waving his arms. "Blay says hi."

The wolf might as well have had springs in his paws the way he was bouncing like a kid on a trampoline.

"Stop," I yelled at him, and…yep. Ordering around an alpha worked about as well as I had figured.

Blay, who must have thought this was a fantastic game, bounded after his friend. Both of them launching into the air, jaws snapping at Dad's heels.

"Back away slowly," Dad growled at Derry, "and I'll return your mate to you."

He was hovering almost above my head, which meant I could now see the problem.

"Marita is shifting." I reached for my magic to zap Derry to attention, but no power answered me. That fast, I had forgotten. Right. No magic. I picked up a rock and hit him between the eyes with it. "Stand down."

Between the frantic chase after his mate, and the direct orders from Dad and me, he was in full-on alpha mode. I don't think Derry could stop and think if he wanted to, and he very much did not want to if the drool stringing his jaw as it snapped shut a foot away from my face was any indication.

Not until spittle hit my cheek did Blay quit playing around and clue in to what was happening.

Above me, Marita finished enough of her transition to speak, and speak she did. At the top of her lungs.

"You *idiot*," she yelled. "You've bit me sixty-five times." She stuck out her (hairy) human leg. "Look at my poor foot." The wolf cocked his head, and I had to agree with him. I didn't see a scratch on her. "I healed it, obviously." She wriggled in Dad's hold. Now that his forearms were locked under her boobs instead of around her wolf's chest, he was starting to look green. "You attacked me. Your *mate*. You're a total idiot."

The wolf bellycrawled to Blay, whining low in his throat in a show of submission few would ever witness from an alpha, even in deference to his mate. Certain Blay would protect him, Derry began his change.

"Yeah." She thrashed against Dad. "You better shift." She blinked, noticing me at last. "Hey!"

"Hey, Marita." I couldn't wipe away my smile. "Mind if Dad puts you down?"

"Not at all." She quit wriggling. "I want a head start."

Poor Derry. He didn't stand a chance. Maybe Dad sensed that and made his descent as slow as possible.

Hands on my hips, I watched the spectacle. "Anyone want to tell me why you got airlifted into camp?"

"Oh." She swung from Dad's grip, landing with a soft thump. "I just wanted to know how it felt to fly."

As I exhaled, my head wilted on my neck. "And Derry was chasing you because…?"

"Saint can only carry one, and I weigh less."

"That…" I was still foggy on the why of it, but sure. "That makes sense."

"Blay would like to fly," he tossed out casually. "Like in Super Mystics."

The commercial for what must be the latest Mystic Realms moneymaker made me snort. Then it hit me. Like a city bus going sixty-five through a crowded pedestrian crosswalk.

Colby isn't here.

Not to put him up to reciting an infomercial.

Not to cackle behind his back like it had been his idea all along.

Not to fly laps around the ceiling, evading capture and a lecture on her spending habits.

"Also?" Marita leaned around me and stuck her tongue out at Derry. "I said upsies first."

As soon as Derry got his legs under him, she ducked past Blay, tackling her mate.

While they wrestled, naked, I decided I would rather be somewhere else. *Anywhere* else. "Dad?"

He trailed after me, still aloft to avoid the wargs, until I reached the edge of the cliff where I had the best view.

Upon spotting the Kellies' helicopter, and its cargo, he landed then joined me with a quizzical brow.

"As much as I love Marita and Derry, I'm not sure why they're here."

"We need their noses." He watched the box sway on its chains. "They're familiar with Clay's scent."

And Colby's, but he and Mom didn't know the full story there yet. "That only matters if we get close."

"Your mother also believes the moral support will help." He cleared his throat. "She's often right."

"She was right." I screwed up my courage to dart in and hug him. "Thanks, Dad."

He settled his hands on my back, soft as a whisper, before I rocked back on my heels to check on the wargs. Their wrestling match had devolved into a make out session. No surprise there.

"The Kellies are our best hope for finding Father." He grimaced as he noticed the Mayhews making up with as much enthusiasm as they had fought. "They know where his safe houses are located and where his personal funds are kept. What they don't know, they can speculate enough to discover."

"I'm counting on it." I rubbed my chest, over the dormant Hunk. "Clay is smart and clever and…"

"I'm sorry." Dad shifted his weight but decided against another embrace. "I know he was your friend."

"*Is*." I curled my fingers into my palms. "Not *was*."

"You can't trust him." He settled for resting a hand on my shoulder. "He's not himself."

"I'm aware." I had seen Clay through times like these over and over again. "I'm not giving up on him."

"Of course you're not." A smile hooked up one side of his mouth. "Neither would your mother."

The reminder I hadn't seen her had me craning my neck, searching for her. "Where is Mom?"

"Meg is drafting the contract for Calixta." He lowered his arm. "Your mother is assisting."

A swirl of complex emotions spun through me as it sank in this was what it meant to have parents. Good parents. People who loved you no matter what. I was lucky to have them. To get this chance to forge the relationship we could have had if the director hadn't ruined all our lives in one fell swoop.

"Everyone has a job." I angled my face toward him. "Except for me."

"Your job is to stay alive until we can unbind your magic."

"I can't sit on the sidelines." I gazed out across the sea. "I have to do something, or I'll go insane."

"That's why I'm here."

"To babysit me so I can't run off and do something stupid?"

"Children are more likely to rebel against their parents than their friends." He brushed an errant curl out of his eyes. "Your friends are more than happy to protect you, even from yourself."

"Okay." I dragged out the word. "What does that leave for you to do?"

"Not me." He cut me a look. "*Us*."

"A father-daughter mission. I like it. What are *we* going to do?"

"We're going to destroy that dark artifact before it destroys you." His wings unfurled on a fetid breeze. "And, if we have time left after that, find Luca and stop her before she exposes our world to humans."

"Blay come too." His appearance startled me as he slung his arm around my shoulders. "Keep Rue safe."

Inclining his head, Dad showed him respect that warmed me. "I would expect nothing less."

"Rue's dad?" He raised his arms over his head. "Upsies."

As Dad's lips parted on an answer that would surely break Blay's heart, I elected to negotiate.

"Once around the camp?" I pleaded with Dad. "That gives me time to make the rounds before we go."

"All right." Dad drew his wand with a thoughtful expression. "How do you feel about mice?"

"Blay like bunnies." He made long ears behind his head with his fingers. "Blay fly now?"

Faster than I could tell Dad to watch where he was pointing that thing, he tapped the end of Blay's nose, transforming him into a crimson bunny with black rosettes. The bunny's burnt-crimson eyes swiveled up to me, and he leapt into my arms.

"You turned him into a bunny." I stroked his velvety fur. "A *bunny*."

"A mouse would have fit in my pocket," Dad lamented. "Either way, he's easier to carry now."

"Are you sure you want to go through with this?" I lifted Blay to eye level, searching for signs of distress. "Twitch your nose once for yes and twice for no."

His adorable nose twitched a mile a minute, which told me nothing.

"We'll be fine." Dad took him from me and tucked him under one arm. "Hurry back."

On my way to update my lieutenants, I stumbled across Derry and Marita.

They paused their whatever they were doing to sniff in my general direction, and I parted my lips.

"I smell…" Derry wet his lips, his eyes flashing gold, "…a bunny."

Snapping my mouth shut, I decided that was why Dad hadn't turned Marita into a prey animal for transport.

"Touch that bunny and die." I kept walking. "And get ready to run."

"We're leaving?" He palmed Marita's forehead and shoved her back. "I call upsies!"

"Too late." I hid my smile as his face fell. "I'm flying AirDad this time."

The reminder I couldn't summon wings for myself was enough to wipe away my amusement too.

This whole magicless thing really and truly sucked.

CHAPTER THREE

*D*ividing me from the Hunk had never been a priority. Too many other emergencies had crowded it out. I wasn't surprised that what bumped it from *I really should get around to this* to *mayday, mayday* was the loss of my magic. The vulnerable didn't survive in our world, and I was now as helpless as any human on the street. Except I had the added bonus of powerful enemies to match my former black witch status.

Clutching the crimson bunny against my chest as Dad flew, I asked, "Where are we going?"

And yes, Blay had suckered me into carrying him on four legs using his newfound weapons. Liquid bunny eyes and a fluffy cotton tail. Derry and Marita weren't thrilled to miss out—on the transmogrification or on the flight—but I didn't trust the gold in their eyes when they looked at Blay's silky fur.

"I have an acquaintance worth visiting. He might have an idea how to nullify the Hunk."

Hope I might access my magic soon buoyed me, and I cuddled Blay closer for the duration of the flight.

An hour after leaving ground zero, we set down on a dirt road leading onto a rickety covered truss bridge painted in shades of red that curled from its weather-beaten planks.

"Your *acquaintance* lives there?" I scanned the area, but there was only the one structure, and the erosion of the road convinced me no one had driven this way in years. "Bridge troll?"

"He's half black witch and half bridge troll, yes."

"Maybe transform Blay?" Not that it would do me any good in my current state, but the urge to reach for my wand while in the presence of another black witch was overwhelming. I would feel safer when Blay was less vulnerable. "I don't want him thinking we brought him a snack."

"Hiram, old friend."

A man, sort of, climbed up from the riverbank. He had the right shape for a witch, but his skin was gray as stone and cut through with cracks. Lichen speckled his cheeks like an acne outbreak, or maybe freckles. His eyes were the dark green of growing things, clear and bright, and they crinkled as they swept over Dad.

"Horatio Proctor." Dad curved his lips, but his gaze remained distant. "It's been too long."

Proctor.

The name clanged through my memory like a wrung bell.

"I thought you were dead." Horatio chortled then crested the rise and spotted me. "Hello, child."

The sweep of his tongue across his lips confirmed I still read as a witch to others of my kind. He must be ravenous to size me up as a potential meal with Dad right beside me. Yet more proof he didn't get many visitors out this far.

"This is my daughter, Rue." Dad's expression darkened, hardened into pure menace. "Put your tongue back in your mouth, or I will rip it out of your head and strangle you with it."

"Daughter?" Horatio wiped the back of his wrist across his mouth. "That would explain how she created a dark artifact on *accident*." His assessment turned curious but no less hungry. "The rest of us should be so lucky." He noticed the bunny and placed a hand over his heart.

"You *did* bring me a gift." He reached for Blay, his fingernails as hard as flint. "How kind."

"Touch the bunny and die." I tightened my grip on Blay, caught Dad's warning expression, then cleared my throat. "And thanks for offering to help."

"Dark artifacts aren't born every day." Proctor's ravenous gaze lingered on the bunny, who flashed his…fangs? "Rarer still are those who can create them." He lost their staring contest. "We didn't know your father was such a one either." His envy flushed his cheeks. "Not until he gave birth to the Maudit Grimoire."

Cold dread trickled down my spine, but I wanted to hear him confirm it. "You know about the grimoire?"

"Know about it?" His indulgent smile revealed algae-green teeth. "I helped *write* it."

"Your father is the only author still alive."

That was what Meg had told me, and she wouldn't have lied to me.

"I was under the impression Dad was the only surviving author."

"I slumbered for a time." Proctor tugged a gray-green lichen off his cheek. "It's the troll in me."

"I see."

"I can fall asleep in the shade one afternoon and wake up as a rock five years later." He dusted the front of an old linen shirt streaked with dirt that appeared to have been worn for several days. "Six months ago, I woke up as part of a water feature in a…" he twisted his wrist, "…sub-di-vi-sion." He wrinkled his nose. "I stank of chemicals, humanity, and canine urine." He glanced around. "It's good to be home."

The book was filled with lethal spells Dad had purged from his mind to prevent himself from becoming a monster. He didn't regret his choice. He made it for Mom, and for me. For our family. For our future. But I could see how, if he hadn't been confined to a cell for so much of my life, his hatred might have turned to resolve to hunt down the grimoire and devour the magic he had once sacrificed and take his revenge.

Proctor claimed to have been sleeping, which might have fooled

Meg into thinking he was dead. Maybe. But the long years he spent without the magic he fed to the book, and his avarice when he learned what I had created, left me concerned he might want his pages back. Worse. He might want them *all*.

Angling toward Dad, I wished I had some privacy to quiz him. "How did you know he was alive?"

"I could sense him." He hesitated, as if loathe to admit the rest. "Through you."

"Through the book, he means." Proctor slid his gaze down my body slowly. "A piece of me is inside you."

Ick.

How had Dad put up with this sleazeball long enough to extract his chapter of information?

The bunny, who Proctor seemed to have forgotten about, leapt from my arms onto his face. He raked the slender black claws on his hind legs across Proctor's cheek, tearing furrows in his grayed flesh, then sank his fangs into the side of his knobby throat. The whole attack lasted seconds, but when Blay kicked off of his chest and sprung into my arms, he was smeared with a different sort of crimson.

"Why you little—" Proctor, who had begun to lunge at me, pulled up short. "What's that I smell?"

"The end of the world as you know it," Marita said from behind me, "if you don't back the fuck off Rue."

The wolf who padded beside her, teeth flashing and eyes golden, spooked Proctor into stepping back.

As much as I appreciated the quick save, we had to be careful how I presented myself around him. If my friends kept fighting my battles for me, he would start to wonder why I wasn't defending myself. I wasn't sure how much Dad had told him about my condition, but I wasn't going to volunteer anything he didn't already know.

"Wargs." Proctor licked his lips. "They're quite good with proper seasoning."

A low rumble poured out of Derry, and Proctor blanched as the wolf stepped in front of his mate.

"Make you a deal." Marita rubbed Derry's ears. "Help my friend, and we'll hunt for you when you're done. We can guarantee you a deer apiece. Maybe one black bear. Possibly a cougar. Your choice."

"Delightful." Proctor eyed the bunny warily. "Set *that* aside, and we'll begin."

After the looks Derry and Marita had shot the bunny, I elected to entrust Blay into Dad's care.

"May I see the artifact?" Proctor crowded my personal space. "A pendant, if I recall correctly?"

With no magic to feed on, the Hunk was pliant when I tugged on the chain, fishing out the gaudy ruby.

"Hello, there." Avarice brightened his eyes. "Do you mind...?"

"Be careful." I held it out so he wouldn't touch my skin. "It's protective of me."

"It's dormant." He flexed his fingers as if debating with himself. "I ought to be fine."

"Suit yourself."

A vestigial twinge prickled through me as the Hunk protested his touch. Or, since he was another author, maybe the reaction was worse. Say, rousing his embedded powers, calling them to the surface.

When it didn't punish him, just lay quiescent, he shut his eyes and cocked his head as if listening.

"I hear my magic calling to me, but it's faint. I can't understand what it's trying to tell me." A deep groove appeared between his brows. "There's...a barrier." He opened his eyes on Dad. "Your doing, Hiram?"

"Focus on the artifact." Dad's voice came out cold. "The rest doesn't concern you."

"They might be one and the same." Proctor rubbed his thumb over the pendant. "There's a connection."

The Hunk had been feeding off me, so, yes. We were connected. Without my magic, though, it was inert.

"Explain this to me." He didn't take his eyes off the pendant. "I must know the ingredients."

On the edge of my periphery, Dad nodded that I could tell him, but

I had to work up to speaking about it to someone new. I was so used to hiding it, protecting it, *avoiding* thinking about it, I had trouble picking a place to start. One that wouldn't give more than I got in return for sharing.

"The pendant was home to a djinn, but it's been vacant for decades. I decided to store the grimoire in it. I was able to call it out and return it without a problem for a while." I didn't see a way around admitting I had added one final element. By accident. But still. "My grandmother-in-law knitted me a Tinkkit choker. Its gift was protection." More or less. "The moment the choker touched the pendant's chain, they fused. I couldn't call the grimoire after that, and I couldn't remove the pendant. Anyone who tried to remove it for me got zapped. Anyone who tried to hurt me, well, they got dead. Whether that was my intention or not."

"I saw the aftermath of one such incident," Dad told Proctor. "She vaporized a coven of black witches."

"What a terrible waste of food." Proctor did glance up then, to frown at me. "How many did you kill?"

The pendant did it. Not me. I'm not to blame.

That was what I wanted to say, but it was a cop-out.

"Enough," I rasped, recalling the sense of helplessness in the aftermath of the slaughter.

The answer didn't please him, but it did appear to amuse him. "You're death averse for a black witch."

I'm not a black witch. Not anymore. I'm a gray witch.

Yet another facet of my power I couldn't risk explaining to him without endangering Colby.

No black witch had ever forged a familiar bond with a *loinnir*, as far as I could tell.

Most would rather eat the *loinnir* for immediate gratification than bind their life to its ephemeral existence.

"I am my father's daughter," I assured him, letting him see in my face I had no problem killing to survive.

"You would have to be," he mused, "to harness the power of your creation."

Dad, who had shifted closer during the evaluation, demanded, "Can you help or not?"

"Are you sure you want to remove it?" Proctor aimed the question at me. "You could be magnificent."

"I could be its puppet," I corrected him. "The artifact wants to control me. It wants to absorb me too."

That was the only word that fit how it had burrowed into the tender flesh between my breasts. I had no idea if or when it would have stopped if Dad hadn't bound my magic to release its stranglehold on me.

"Fascinating." His gaze went unfocused in a way that reminded me of how Dad spaced out to view spells and the threads that knotted them together. "I'm not sure if it's a comfort," he said moments later, "but the sentience is an extension of the book. The other objects are channeling its will." He blinked away the blankness in his stare. "They have none of their own." He shook his head. "The grimoire alone was a feat of mastery, but this? This is artistry. Does this configuration allow you to access the book's pages? Does it whisper its secrets to you?"

"I see what it wants to show me." I kept darting glances at Dad. "It has a mind of its own."

"Let me think on it." He lowered the pendant with reverence. "I would like it intact, if possible."

"What about me?"

"I'll see what I can do." He withdrew a few steps. "Come back to see me tomorrow."

"We don't have that kind of time," I protested, as concern for Colby flared within me. "Can you do this or not?"

"Do this for us," Dad offered Proctor, "and I will be in your debt."

"An unspecified favor from the great Hiram Nádasdy is not worth nothing." Proctor angled toward his bridge with an odd longing, as if it hurt him to stand even this far away from it. "Give me a half hour."

"All right." Dad locked a hand on my shoulder before I could protest. "We'll take a short walk."

Halfway back to his bridge, Proctor raised a hand in farewell as he hustled toward its dank shade.

Using his grip on me, Dad aimed me at the woods and nudged me into a brisk walk.

Marita and Derry followed until the bridge was almost out of sight then hid in the overgrowth to watch over Proctor. They must have worried, like me, that he would call for reinforcements or plot some other way to take the Hunk from me. Probably my head too, while he was at it. And my heart. Why waste free food?

"How long have you known where to find him?"

"I found him three days ago. As soon as I read your magic, I could tell the thread he had woven into the grimoire burned as bright as mine. I suspected then that the book was feeding on him in some way. Which meant he was alive. Perhaps dormant but alive. That was when I began searching."

"And you didn't tell me this sooner because...?"

"Proctor didn't want to participate in the grimoire. His partner, Edward, convinced him they had enough magic between them that they could afford to part with a little. Edward was a black witch but not a very good one. He didn't have the stomach for it. I believed then Edward longed to save Proctor in the same way your mother wanted to save me."

As we walked, Dad began scratching Blay's ears, but it was an absent gesture as his thoughts meandered through the past.

The condition we found Proctor in spoke for itself, but I asked anyway. "Are they still together?"

"Edward was killed not long after we completed the grimoire. Another black witch cut out his heart."

Yep. I had been right to dread the answer. No surprise there. Love and black witches didn't mix.

"That's why Proctor went to sleep." I couldn't say I blame him. "He had no reason to stay awake."

"Without Edward, he has no reason to hold back." Dad delivered the news with the bite of a guillotine blade. "Proctor will want his magic returned to him."

"I picked up on that," I said dryly.

"Asking Proctor for help was a last resort." Dad continued petting the bunny. "I don't trust him, and I don't trust him to be useful, but these are desperate times."

A buzz in my pocket sent me reaching for my phone to read a text from Isiforos.

>>*Witches have finished warding Ballroom Three. Kellies are en route.*

>*Get them plugged in and ready to work ASAP.*

>>*Will do, boss.*

"We're still looking at a couple of hours until the Kellies get settled and start searching for the director." I thumped my phone across my palm. "I hate this." I wrapped my hand around the pendant and yanked out of frustration. "I could find my familiar if I could sense her." I wet my lips. "It might be worth—"

"The book will consume you if it gets a foothold in your power again." He pried the ruby from my hand. "No familiar is worth your life."

That was where he was wrong. Colby and my lives were intertwined. But to explain my desperation to reach her, I would have to give my parents more of my story. That presented its own complications.

Better to press the angle that, through her, we could track Clay's—and therefore the director's—movements.

Under orders, Clay had the personality of a wet paper bag. He became an empty vessel, a blank slate, and it gutted me to watch how it whittled him down to a bare-bones version of himself I didn't recognize as my best friend.

Clay would do everything in his power to protect Colby, to get her back to me. But the golem? The shell? She didn't matter to him. Her fate wasn't his problem. He wouldn't care if she lived or if she died.

A shimmer distorted the air, and a figure limned in soft blue light appeared before us.

"Mom?" I reached out and touched her, expecting my fingers to pass through, but she felt solid. "How did you do that?"

"Your father made me a teleportation charm." She lifted her wrist to display a thin row of small pearls. "I can only travel to him then return to my point of origin, but where else would I want to be?"

She winked at him when she said it, and that somehow warmed me. I let myself enjoy the grossness of having parents who still flirted with each other then made retching noises to do Clay proud.

"Yuck." I wiped the back of my hand across my mouth. "I thought you were with Meg, working on the contract for Calixta."

"We're in the thick of it." Her expression reflected my own frustration at how much time we didn't have. "I came to check on my two great loves while she consults a daemon colleague on some obscure law."

While Meg kept up to date on the ever-evolving legal system from beyond the veil, she required help for the physical job of purchasing new books, turning pages, writing notes. That sort of thing. She employed an army of paralegals across realms, factions, and species.

"I'm fine." I heard in my voice how not-fine I was, and she must have too. "I just want Clay back."

And Colby.

Goddess, I missed my little girl.

I would do anything, *anything* to get her home safely.

Even if it was the last thing I ever did.

CHAPTER FOUR

*C*olby

I CAN'T BREATHE, I CAN'T BREATHE, I CAN'T BREATHE.

"Calm down," I ordered myself in my best Rue-like voice. "There are holes in the lid. I *can* breathe. I have air, a sugar cube, and a soda bottle lid full of water."

I locked down my twitching wings before instinct launched me into another spin around the jar I was trapped in. Beating myself against the glass didn't help. It just gave me a headache.

"Moth?"

The golem, who was and wasn't Clay, must have heard me and peeked into his suit jacket where he kept the jar close to where his heart would be.

A lump welled in my throat, but I wouldn't cry. I wasn't a baby. I was Captain Colby of the *Scurvy Dog*. What would my team think if they saw me break on my first day as a captive? I wasn't even being interrogated. This was pathetic. I couldn't let them down.

"Moth cry?"

Barnacles, I cursed to myself. I couldn't stop hot tears from pouring down my cheeks. Not when he looked at me with Clay's eyes in Clay's face and spoke in Clay's voice. Except his speech was all wrong.

The golem wasn't clever or quick like Clay. He wasn't dumb or slow. He was just *wrong, wrong, wrong*.

Every time he spoke to me, I could tell the words took effort. They got caught in his mouth sometimes, like he wasn't supposed to say them. Or think them.

"I want to go home." I sniffled, sort of. I didn't have a nose anymore. "I want Rue."

"Rue," he said thoughtfully, a film covering his eyes, and he didn't move for the longest time.

He did that too. Froze. Just stopped. Like he was a wind-up toy that had run out of key turns.

The real Clay was never still. He was always moving, always laughing, always smiling. He was *alive*.

"Hush," he breathed, animating once more, and closed his jacket with a snap of his wrist.

As darkness fell, the door groaned on its hinges, and that weird *step, step, thump* noise approached us.

"Are the preparations in order?"

Holding my breath, I hoped he would explain what preparations, but he held out longer than me.

"The safehouse in Charlotte is secure," the golem said, able to speak clearly when asked a direct question by the man, who must have been Rue's scary grandfather. "The condo in Dallas is also freshly warded and ready for your arrival."

Charlotte?

Dallas?

I could remember those cities. I *would* remember. As soon as I got back to Rue, I would tell her.

"Bjorn was always so meticulous," he lamented then sighed. "We leave within the hour."

"Yes, Master."

Step, step, thump.

Step, step, thump.

Step, step, thump.

The door protested as it closed behind the director. *Former* director. I wasn't sure what to call him.

Names held power.

My mom taught me that…before.

He didn't deserve my fear. No one did.

Rue taught me that.

There was a big bad in Mystic Seas that I hated with the fire of a thousand suns. Big Nose Baron. I bet the director would flip if he heard me call him that. I couldn't picture his face—I had never seen it —but I could imagine a grumpy old man scowling at me while his cheeks turned as red as a shark bite.

Big Nose Baron, it is.

"Clay?" I pitched my voice low. "Can I ask you something?"

The golem didn't answer, just continued his task, leaving me to sit and stare into the dark.

CHAPTER FIVE

*M*om left within minutes of her arrival, which was for the best. Proctor was salivating over the grimoire. I didn't want to watch him drool over Mom like she was a juicy steak he couldn't wait to bite. One wrong word, and Dad would gut him. That would be that. Any help he could offer me would die with him.

Having walked a loop, Dad and I circled back to the covered bridge to hear the verdict.

The Mayhews fell in step behind us, Marita having shifted back onto four legs to roam with Derry.

I didn't have much hope left in me, so I wasn't surprised when Proctor gave no hint of having experienced a revelation.

"To separate her from the artifact," he announced without flourish, "we'll have to kill her."

One second, Proctor stood before me. The next, he dangled from Dad's hand where his fingers latched around his fellow author's throat.

"Touch my daughter and die."

Huh.

Dad and I had more in common than I would have thought.

We both used the same death threat.

"I'm not…proposing…we let her…stay…dead." Proctor wriggled and thrashed. "We could—"

"No." Dad bit off the word with a click of his teeth. "Do you have a solution or not?"

The quiver in his upper lip would have done any warg proud, and the Mayhews followed suit.

"Put him down." I patted Dad's shoulder to soften the order. "Let him speak."

So far, we were two for two on killing me to break my connection with the Hunk. Not great odds. I knew Asa's grandmother had my best interests at heart. This guy? Not so much. I wanted to hear his reasons.

"Another expert I consulted expressed concerns the artifact might view my death as a sacrifice. That it might grow more sentient as a result." I grimaced as a fire lit within his gaze. "What do you think?"

"I confess—" Proctor coughed then rubbed his throat, "—it's a possibility."

"How likely is it?" I watched him consider his answer. "Spit it out, or I'll let Dad finish the interrogation."

"I would give it a seventy-five percent chance of increasing in power." His tongue darted across his lips. "If you were to say, bleed out on it, after I slit your throat, that would shift the odds closer to ninety."

A high-pitched scream was all the warning Bunny Blay gave before launching himself at Proctor.

This time, I was close enough to catch him midleap by the scruff and pin him against my chest.

"What's wrong with that demon beast?" Proctor backed away. "Is it possessed?"

"He's a *daemon*, actually." I nodded to Dad then set Blay on the ground. "Do you mind?"

Crouching over Blay, Dad stroked his hand down the bunny's spine, leaving a ripple of fire in its wake.

"Now that's better." Proctor leaned in. "Chargrilled rabbit is delicious."

As the flames rose, creating a bonfire, Blay emerged in his usual hulking form with a vicious smile.

"Rock man touch Rue, Blay kill him." His expression softened on me. "Like otdrels."

Apparently, Blay was also a fan of the old standby. A gold standard in threats, really. A true classic.

"O-o-otdrels?" Proctor cringed away from Blay. "This *thing* hunts otdrels?"

"This *thing* is the love of my life." A growl entered my voice. "Watch yourself."

I knew I had made a mistake the second the words left my mouth, and Blay began preening.

"Rue love Blay more than Asa." He handed me a section of his hair. "Asa wish Asa was Blay, but Asa not Blay. Sucks to be Asa."

While I did my duty, stroking my fingers through his sleek hair, I nudged Proctor. "Well?"

While he had a healthy fear of Dad that was plain to see, Dad was a less imposing figure with his golden, cherubic curls and fitted clothes. Sometimes, with an enemy, a visual reminder of impending doom worked wonders.

"You don't understand." Proctor darted glances between Dad and Blay, and his fear left me curious how much of his magic was tied up in the grimoire for him to be so afraid of them and yet so willing to kill me to preserve it. "The only other option would result in destroying the artifact."

"The artifact will be destroyed either way," Dad told him, and there was no give in his tone.

"You can't do that." Proctor bristled. "You can't neuter me for the rest of my life."

"You gave up those spells, that magic, willingly. I haven't done anything to you. You agreed to the terms."

"It's not the same for you," he exploded. "You're the strongest of us, even without the parts of yourself you bled out onto the page. You can afford to give up those pieces. I can't. Not anymore."

"If the choice is power or my daughter, I will always choose my child."

"What kind of father would allow his child to fall into this trap in the first place?" Proctor laughed, its edge cutting. "You should have taught her better, if you wanted her to survive our world."

The barb struck Dad with the force of a blow, and he turned his cheek as if Proctor had slapped him.

The thing about the Maudit Grimoire was I thought it was the *Proctor* Grimoire for a while. Until I learned of its many authors, including Dad. The section Proctor wrote was the first thing it showed me. That was how I came across his name. But it hadn't occurred to me, except in an abstract way, that he had written the portions on *loinnir*. How to make them, and how to consume them.

With that in mind, his desperation to reclaim that knowledge made far more sense. It also convinced me that Proctor had truly loved Edward since he had been willing to bow to his wishes at such personal cost.

The grimoire could remind him how he made *loinnir*, and how to grow his power by consuming them. Without Edward's gentling influence, Proctor could spiral if he was allowed to recover that knowledge.

Maybe that was what he wanted so badly. Not power, exactly, but *exponential* power.

As tempting as it was to ask him questions, this person who had once been an expert, it was foolish. The odds of him knowing how to keep a *loinnir* alive and happy, even back when the information was fresh in his head, were nil. I would have to go on as I had been, learning from trial and error.

"Blay kill rock man?" He popped his knuckles. "Blay not mind."

"There's no need." I gave him one last pet. "We're leaving."

After hearing my decision, Dad whipped his head toward me, a pucker between his brows.

"Are you sure?" His expression didn't change. "He's of no use to you?"

"He wants the artifact, and I can't trust him not to kill me to get to it."

"I regret wasting your time in bringing you here." He dipped his chin. "And I apologize for this."

Before I grasped his intentions, he drew his athame and stabbed Proctor in the heart, twisting the blade as the other witch hit his knees then toppled sideways.

The sudden violence shouldn't have shocked me, but I swallowed a gasp at the unexpected brutality.

"He never would have stopped hunting you," Dad said softly, bending to incinerate the body.

"Yeah." I smoothed out the bumps in my voice. "I was starting to see that."

"He wrote the chapters on *loinnir*," he confessed. "That was the secondary reason I agreed to see him."

Much like me with Colby in those early days, Dad was frantic to learn all he could about caring for Mom, but I was beginning to suspect there was another layer to our purpose in coming. That Dad had intended to evaluate the threat Proctor posed and eliminate him if necessary. Whether or not he helped me.

"The book showed me." I smacked my nape to kill a mosquito. "That's how it got to me."

"How it got to you?" He angled his head, studying me. "At Father's cabin?"

The time for half-truths was quickly coming to an end, but I held out for a while longer.

"It shows you what you want more than anything," I hedged, "at the exact time you need it most."

It counted on desperation shoving you across moral lines you wouldn't have crossed without the nudge.

"That's the nature of black magic," he said after a moment where I was sure he would press harder.

"You can't lure people to the dark side without cookies."

If Clay had been here, he would have gotten the joke, but he wasn't, and Dad didn't grasp pop culture.

A warm breath exhaled into my palm as Marita bumped her head under my hand.

She must have sensed, or scented, my twinge of sadness.

When I left the Bureau to protect Colby, I had phantom limb syndrome for years from losing Clay. To get him back? To finally see a way into a future where we could always be together? Truly friends forever? It gutted me to watch all he had worked for begin to crumble. And if he harmed Colby under compulsion? If he became another White Stag nightmare that haunted her? He would never forgive himself.

Derry padded up to my other side and leaned against me, offering his support while Dad watched with a softness in his expression that told me he was thinking of Mom, of how alike we were in some ways. For some reason, it didn't rankle anymore. That he loved her so much.

Given time, which we now had to get to know one another, we had a second chance. All of us. Together.

A text chime sent me searching for my phone, and the number caused my gut to clench.

"Fergal," I told everyone. "Maybe he's got good news from ground zero."

With Isiforos traveling with the Kellies, that left Fergal in charge of Arden and the former compound.

>>*Thirteen humans dead in Charlotte after eating tainted food.*

>*North Carolina? That's a big jump from Massachusetts.*

>>*Not by plane. They're both major airline hubs.*

As tempting as it was to send Fergal to deal with this latest outbreak in my place, I couldn't shake the certainty settling into my bones that I should go too. Premonition wasn't a talent of mine, but I sensed a weight to this decision. I needed to be in Charlotte. I wasn't sure why yet, but I couldn't ignore my surety.

Drawing in a long breath, I made the choice to listen to my inner voice.

>*Leave ground zero in the hands of the team leader.*

>*We'll meet you in Charlotte.*

CHAPTER SIX

THE GOLEM DIDN'T TYPE LIKE CLAY. NOBODY ELSE WOULD NOTICE, BUT I did. The difference made me sad.

Clay was spurts of fingers on keys then stretches of quiet when he got distracted. Usually by food or an email about a sale on wigs or clearance clothes or discounted tech. He was kind of a shopaholic.

The golem was steady and focused and silent.

When he stood and stretched, he peeked into his pocket and checked on me.

"I need to pee," I blurted. "I have to go really bad."

"You're a moth."

"I'm a little girl spelled to look like a moth."

That wasn't the truth anymore, but this version of Clay didn't know any better.

"Bathroom?" He massaged his throat as words became harder for him to wrangle. "Toilet?"

"Yes." I fluttered my wings. "Let me out, and I'll go straight there and come straight back."

For a moment, he studied me, his expression slipping and sliding on his face. Then he examined his room with the same focus. He stood, closed the vents, and stuffed a towel in the crack under the door.

The spark of hope he would underestimate me flickered and died as he finished moth-proofing the room.

With that done, he withdrew the jar and set it on the counter next to the toilet. "Quick."

"Okay." I did the best potty dance I could manage. "Thank you."

The lid unscrewed into his palm, and he watched me climb out and stretch my cramped wings.

"Can I have some privacy?" I rubbed my front legs together. "I'm embarrassed to go in front of you."

A sigh parted his lips, and he turned his back.

I flew until I hovered at his nape, close enough to tell he still smelled like Clay, and drew on my power. As much as I hated to leave him here with Big Nose Baron, I didn't have a choice. Rue couldn't save him if she didn't know where to find him.

"Hurry," he said a moment later, hesitant, as if unsure how long a moth required to tinkle.

Sadly, he had stopped up my preferred exits. That left me with one option. A dangerous one. But it wasn't like I was safe here. Not with the BNB next door.

Tub drain, it is.

"I love you," I mouthed to his back then climbed down the pipe into the dark.

CHAPTER SEVEN

Fergal and Arden left ahead of us, but we weren't far behind. The flight was quick, but the cost was high. And I don't just mean the rush tickets for everyone minus Dad, who preferred his wings to the ones on the plane. The twenty-four hours I started with were dwindling fast.

Realistically, I had known I couldn't meet the deadline with Calixta the second Isiforos broke the news.

As it turns out, *knowing* a thing and *accepting* it are two different things.

The centuria had begun staging nonlethal skirmishes on Hael's borders, but Calixta hadn't reached out. To either of us. Them to broker peace or us to make apologies for bumping back our meeting while she handled the threat to her rule. There was the time difference to consider. I hoped that was the problem.

Please let that be the problem.

The faster the sand ran from the hourglass, the more frantic my heart banged in my chest, urging me to *go, go, go*. I spent the whole flight with sweaty palms, which Asa was kind enough not to mention while he held my hand. I was first in line off the plane, grateful to stretch my legs and burn off nervous energy.

From the grunts and muttered curses, the others were elbowing their way to me through the crowd.

"I smell Arden." Marita's eyes sparkled bright. "And...fish tacos." Her eyes turned dreamy. "Mmm."

"We're not here to eat." Derry made heart eyes at a pizza shop. "We're here to work."

"Get what you want but get it to go." I shooed them toward the food. "Find us when you're done."

The courier angle Luca had been working wouldn't fly in an airport, so the food ought to be safe.

Asa and I headed for baggage claim, not that we had any, but that was our agreed upon meeting point.

Sure enough, Arden waited for us behind a metal barrier set in place to herd passengers away from an ongoing construction project. She carried a drink holder full of frosty beverages in pastel tones that made my heart squeeze with memories of simpler times when I had sipped smoothies for breakfast on my way to work at Hollis Apothecary.

"Fergal said the food here is fine." She held up the tray. "Airport security is a little tighter than what Luca is comfortable with." She pointed to each cup. "Strawberry banana swirl, peaches and cream, and orange creamsicle." She passed us each a straw. "Not the most inventive flavors, but they're classics. I figured we couldn't go wrong with them."

"Thanks." I reached for what I thought was orange creamsicle and slurped hard. "Peaches and cream."

Asa, who had taken the other orangey-cream striped drink, offered his to me. "Trade?"

"You just want my straw," I teased, a bittersweet twinge reminding me of when he wouldn't eat unless I took a bite of his food first. We had progressed beyond that point in our courtship, and I missed it often. "I'm so tired, I can't taste. You can keep the orange."

"Fergal?" Asa stole my drink and replaced it with his before I could fuss. "He sent you to fetch us alone?"

The sun was up now, so he hadn't had much choice.

"Um, no." Arden shifted her weight. "He's out in the SUV we had dropped off by a local agent."

"That tracks." I swallowed too fast and got a brain freeze. "He worries about you."

"I like him." Her cheeks pinked. "He's like a cooler, deadlier uncle than Uncle Nolan."

The mystery of what happened to Nolan barely rated a slot on my endless to-do list, but I would have to tell Arden what I suspected one day. Namely that he got in over his head after discovering the existence of paranormal creatures. As a wildlife photographer, it had opened up a whole new world to him. I had a gut feeling documenting what wished to remain hidden hadn't gone well for him.

We would have to talk about him eventually, and the truth would go down easier if I had all the details.

"Uncle Fergie." I had to say it since Clay wasn't here to do it for me. "It has a nice ring to it."

A flush overtook her face as Marita and Derry joined us, their arms overflowing with bagged food.

"This is for you." She smacked a bag into my chest. "Eat it, or I'll tell Clay you starved yourself, got low blood sugar, and that's how you ended up with that tragic tattoo."

Fingers curling around the paper, I was afraid to ask, "What tragic tattoo?"

"Exactly." She pointed a warning finger at me. "Now eat." She hit Asa with his own bag. "You too."

"Where to next?" Derry bit into a slice of pizza as big as his head. "Where's Fergal?"

"The barracks are our next stop." I investigated my haul. "Fergal is waiting in the SUV."

The four of us followed Arden out, toddling like baby ducks behind our momma as we crammed in food. I got beef and onion stuffed dumplings that tasted fresh out of a microwave, but I liked it that way. I felt guilty eating good food without sharing it with Clay. This stuff? Yeah. No guilt whatsoever. It was fuel. Plain and simple.

The text chime in my pocket made me wish I had something stiffer than a smoothie to drink.

>>*The Kellies are secure.*

"It's Isiforos." I had been bracing for word the body count had risen. "The Kellies are secure."

>*Excellent.*

Now I had to choose. Put them both on the poisoning case? Split them up? Set Kelly on Luca and Kelley on the director? *Former* director. As the current director, my agents ought to be my top priority. Preserving the secret existence of paranormal creatures should rank as a solid number two. But Clay was family, and Colby...

"Breathe." Asa drew me into his arms, bent his head to mine, and whispered, "It's going to be okay."

"Which part? Finding Colby before she gets hurt? Finding Clay before he does something he can't forgive himself for? Finding the director? Or giving him to Calixta? Stopping Luca and her insane murder spree?"

"If we miss the deadline with Calixta, we'll figure out a counteroffer she can't refuse." He rightly guessed that was the most pressing matter on my mind behind the all-consuming fear for Colby. "The rest? We can handle. All of us. Together."

I had to set aside my heart and *think*.

What was best for the Bureau?

Luca was the active threat. To more than my family. To us all. She was killing humans. In droves.

The director was a passive threat, for now, while he licked his wounds.

That meant...I had made my decision.

Withdrawing from the comfort of Asa's embrace, I willed my thumbs to get typing on my phone.

>*Put the Kellies to work finding Luca.*

>*We need to squash that problem before she exposes us all.*

>>*I'll keep you updated.*

"Contact the centuria remaining at the farm. Draft us an aerial scout." I locked eyes with Asa as I put away my cell. "I want eyes in the skies over The Spinnaker."

Now that we had the Kellies, I didn't want to risk losing them. A warded room did not a prison cell make.

"Let us know if you need extra paws on the ground," Marita said, a growl in her voice and food in her teeth. "We can draft a few packmates."

"Yeah." Derry gazed at her as if she were a full moon on a cloudless night, dark and mysterious and hauntingly beautiful. He didn't even blink when she bit down too hard and choked on the stick from her corn dog. "What she said."

"Thanks." I blew out a sigh. "I'll let you know if we need to call in that favor."

With that settled, everyone packed into the SUV, most of us sorting ourselves into our usual slots.

Asa drove. I rode shotgun. Arden sat on the bench.

But this time, Arden shared with Marita and Derry instead of Clay and Colby. Fergal had taken the Mayhews' usual spot in the cargo area, where he waited in the heavy body bag he traveled in, tucked under a blanket.

"Fergal." I heard the zipper drag as soon as the doors shut. "Who reported the deaths?"

"Sergeant Londis of the CPD." Fergal crinkled as he shifted. "He's a boojum, a relation of the sasquatch."

I recalled Captain Peters' advice about how I needed to address our allies and let them know the Bureau had their backs, that our agents were under control. She had been championing Boston, her hometown, but this was as good a time as any to put her theory to the test in other cities.

"I want to meet Londis, reassure him I have everything under control, and convince him to let the Bureau handle this." I peered out my window, but Dad wouldn't be here for a while yet. "Then Dad and I will hole up somewhere and see if we can think of a way to remove the Hunk. Without killing me."

The longer we waited, the more tempted I became to risk powering up once more.

All I need is five minutes to know where to find them.

"All the Hunk needs is five minutes," Asa said, "to finish what it started with that scar on your chest."

"I didn't mean to say that part out loud."

Just as I hadn't meant to rest a hand over the tender ridges of skin between my breasts.

"You didn't." He frowned at the ruby pendant. "I could tell it was what you were thinking."

"Mate mind powers." Derry ruffled my hair. "The longer you're together, the less you can hide from one another."

"Thanks for the warning." I didn't miss Asa's sigh. "Not that I would hide anything, mind you."

"Of course not." Marita backed me up with a grin. "That would be wrong."

"Like you never hide anything from me." Derry huffed. "Don't lie to our friends."

"I would *never*."

Their bickering faded to a background noise that oddly comforted until a call drew my attention. "Hollis."

"…me…"

"You're breaking up." I prepared to end the call. "Try back later."

"…it's *me*…"

Adrenaline flooded my veins, and magic or no magic, I could have fought a giant and won right then.

"Colby?" I could taste my heartbeat in my throat. "Where are you?"

"…Clay…" A crackling fuzz boiled down the connection. "…Charlotte…"

"You're in Charlotte?" I reached for my magic, eager to check our bond, but of course nothing answered me. Only the emptiness in my chest. But I had known. Maybe not that she was here, but that I had to be. I wasn't sure what it meant, but it had to mean something. "Where are you?"

"…flight…arriving…six."

"Six tonight or six tomorrow?"

"I…night…at six."

"I'll meet you at the airport." I couldn't see. "At six." Stupid tears blinded me. "Okay?"

Another buzz and a louder whirr, and the call dropped, leaving me clutching a blank screen.

"I thought…" I sucked in air. "I don't know what I thought."

Yes, I did. That I had lost her. Forever.

"Colby is clever and resourceful. She's a survivor." Asa drew me across my seat, until my hip bumped the console, and guided my head onto his shoulder. "I'm not surprised she's fighting her way back to you."

"Do you think Clay…?" I clenched my eyes shut. "He couldn't have helped her, even if he wanted to."

As hard as I wished this was proof my best friend was still in there, I had never seen any evidence to support he was aware while functioning in this altered state.

Burying my face in Asa's neck, I couldn't hold back the sobs any longer as my heart cracked wider and fickle hope teased the ragged edges with a promise I would soon be whole again.

CHAPTER EIGHT

The Golem

MOTH GONE. FLEW DOWN PIPE.

    Away from the golem.

    Away from Master.

    The golem watched her. Saw her in the mirror.

    He should have. Stopped her. Caught her. Given her to Master.

    So.

    Much.

    Power.

    But he heard her. Talk to Clay. Tell him she…

    …loved him.

    No one loved the golem.

    But this moth. She loved Clay. And the golem…

    …he was Clay sometimes.

    Wasn't he?

CHAPTER NINE

*W*ith two hours before Colby's flight landed, I fought the urge to shirk my duties and sit in the airport with my nose pressed against the glass while I waited on her plane to land. But I had to deal with Londis.

Easier said than done when the message from Colby plagued me.

How had she called? Had Clay let her? Had she escaped him? How was she getting on a plane?

Clay didn't fly. There was too much of him. Four hundred pounds' worth.

The director was borderline agoraphobic. I doubted he would climb into a metal tube full of strangers, breathe their air, and listen to their chatter of his own free will. It would be torture, and he was a man who preferred his creature comforts.

So then, how was Colby getting here? Was she acting alone? Or was she still in Clay's custody?

As usual, I had more than enough questions to last me a lifetime and no answers whatsoever.

Fear for her was a tornado spinning through my head, scattering thoughts like debris when I needed my focus on the poisonings.

"We're here." Asa parked at a coffee shop with a frilly pink sign. "Ready?"

Behind him, Arden tracked incoming flights to Charlotte on her cell to give me a false sense of control.

The Mayhews, meanwhile, were engaging in an energetic thumb war over an airport brownie.

Sensing my attention, Arden glanced up at me. "The longest delay is fifteen minutes."

"Thanks," I rasped, my throat tightening at her kindness.

"I see Londis." Asa peered through the windshield at a lean man in a CPD uniform.

"Then it's showtime." I exited the vehicle, Asa beside me. "Do I look trustworthy and professional?"

I hadn't showered in what felt like years, I hadn't brushed my hair, and my clothes were rumpled within an inch of their lives. I didn't have to see my reflection to know my eyes were bloodshot from stress, lack of sleep, and my earlier crying jag.

"You're beautiful." He held the door to the coffee shop for me. "Always."

"You're a liar, but I love you."

The sergeant, who had been nibbling on a black and white cookie, lifted his head as the open door swirled our scents to him. He sipped his coffee and moved to join us, his gait cautious but confident.

Nothing about him screamed *Bigfoot is on my Christmas card list*. He looked perfectly ordinary, perfectly human. Looks, as I well knew, could be deceiving.

"You must be Rue Hollis and Asa Montenegro." He offered us each a cookie from a large white bag, which improved my opinion of him on the spot. Even if he had dropped our titles. "I'm Bryan Londis."

The choice to ignore his rank convinced me he wasn't impolite, just informal.

"That's us." I toasted him with my cookie. "Thanks for making time for us."

"You can eat that, by the way." He demonstrated with gusto. "They don't offer delivery."

To be polite, I bit into the treat, which was a buttery shortbread under sweet royal icing.

Clay would have approved.

When Asa indicated he would fetch us hot drinks, giving me a moment alone with Londis, I nodded. "I take it that means you've read our files on the troubles in Boston."

Londis indicated a table, and we sat across from one another, leaving room for Asa at my elbow.

"I have read your files, thanks to a fellow named Fergal, and we've already isolated footage that leads us to believe the unsub has stuck with what works." He placed his palms on the table. "Level with me here. This Luca. What do you know about her?"

Not much that wouldn't cast Black Hat in a bad light. This was our dirty laundry coming out in the wash.

"She's fae." I started off easy. "She comes from a region of Faerie that grows king killer."

"So, she's got an endless supply then." He cursed then reached for another cookie. "Please continue."

"She's holding a grudge against the former director." I rolled around other possible details to share in the spirit of cooperation. "We believe that's why she's targeting humans."

"Black Hat is dedicated to concealing the existence of supernaturals from human detection." He chewed thoughtfully. "I could see how she might want to subvert that mission to spit in his eye."

I waited a beat, certain the accusations would begin, but he simply reached for another treat.

"I apologize for bringing this to your door." I was thrown off balance by his calmness. "A local black witch coven spread the poison in Boston. I would start looking for her accomplices among any dark practitioners in your city." He kept right on snacking. "You, ah, seem very chill about this."

"You're being open and honest with me. It's the least I can do in return." He reached for another cookie, only to realize the bag was empty. "Here's the thing. In my experience, people with a grudge are looking for an excuse to justify acting on it. If one thing hadn't set off this Luca person, something else would have eventually." He crumpled up the paper. "That, and blame gets us nowhere. This is a matter of protecting the existence of *every* supernatural from discovery. I don't care who caused the problem. It's here now, and we all need to work together to solve it."

Asa set a steaming cappuccino in front of me with a cartoon moth drawn in the froth, and…I didn't get how I could be so lucky. How had I landed him? Seriously. Despite how he had been raised, the guiding influences in his life, he was good right down to the bone. I wished I could say the same.

"These are for you." Asa set one bag of cookies in front of Londis. "And these are for you."

Maybe it was his kindness, his thoughtfulness, or maybe I could let go knowing I was about to hold Colby in my arms. But *feelings* overwhelmed me in a wildfire rush that burned low in my stomach.

"I love you." I peeked in my bag to find snickerdoodles. "And not just because you brought me cookies."

"You guys are a thing?" Londis crammed a chocolate chip cookie into his mouth. "I maybe heard that."

"He's my mate." For me, claiming him never got old. "He's also the new deputy director."

"Aww." Londis sipped his drink. "That's cute."

Another person might have accused Asa of sleeping his way to the top, or me of abusing my privilege as his superior. But not Londis. I decided I liked him and resolved to make a note of him as a reliable point of contact in Charlotte for the next time our troubles crossed state lines in his direction.

"Can you spare the manpower to help us locate any black witches in the area?"

A phone rang, and thankfully, this time, it wasn't mine.

"Londis," he answered with a hand in his cookie bag. "Yeah." His fingers curled in a fist. "Be right there."

Ending the call, he rose, tossed back his coffee in one gulp, and pocketed the remaining cookies.

"I have to go." His friendly expression hardened. "We have three more victims." He held himself back from rushing out the door. "Have your people coordinate with mine. We'll begin a sweep of the city."

"Thank you for your time." I rose and tossed back my drink too. "We'll be in touch."

Alone with Asa in the coffee shop, I drew in a slow breath and exhaled through my nose. The exercise did nothing to soothe my nerves. Probably because my phone chose that moment to ring. "Hollis."

"I have arrived," Dad announced in my ear, twice as loud as a normal person.

"Excellent." The knot in my gut loosened a bit. "We're heading to the airport."

Quickly as possible, I updated him on what he had missed and outlined our plan.

"I'll follow in the air." He kept his voice on blast. "I can patrol the area for signs of trouble."

Without knowing who to expect, or what they had planned, that was all any of us could do.

"Sounds good." I held the phone away from my ear. "See you soon."

"I've arranged for a dozen agents working in pairs to guard the entry and exit points." Asa clearly overheard our conversation. "The Mayhews can join your dad on patrol to cover a wider area."

"Are you sure that's wise?" I disliked agents in such close proximity to Colby. "Can we trust them to stand with us against the director if he shows?"

"We don't have much choice."

"Well, when you put it like that, I see your point." I wished we had more trustworthy agents to fill key roles, and maybe we would one day, but not today. "I'm just…"

"Afraid to hope? Afraid it's a trap? Afraid Colby is a prisoner?"

"You've put a lot of thought into how I'm feeling."

"I'm feeling it too." He meshed our fingers. "Come on." He pulled me toward the door. "Let's bring our girl home."

The airport hadn't changed in the time since we disembarked, and yet *everything* had changed.

This was it. The moment of truth. Colby would be here soon.

The *how* left me in a cold sweat, unsure who she would arrive with and in what condition.

For an hour, those fears gnawed on me like a dog with a hambone, splintering me between its teeth.

The timer I set on my phone for six o'clock chimed, jerking my spine straight and my shoulders back, but there was no sign of her. Or Clay. Or the director. And if they used glamour to conceal themselves?

Well, I would be worthless detecting it, let alone piercing it, without any magic of my own to counter it.

Good thing Asa was here. The Mayhews too. That gave us plenty of sniffing power to root out any active spells. Even in a flurry of activity and smells, black magic's ripe stench wasn't easily ignored.

"Flights run late all the time." Asa slid one arm around my waist. He held Colby's green blanket, the one he had knitted her, in the other. He must have had it retrieved from where she and Clay had been staying. That he didn't also have her laptop told me it had been taken. "We don't know which was hers."

But the board flickering with updates showed no delays for domestic flights for the next three hours.

A teenage girl with curly blue hair swerved out of the line for coffee and trotted up to me. "Rue Hollis?"

Asa flared his nostrils then nodded once to me that it was safe.

"That's me." I kept a wary eye on her. "How can I help you?"

"Calixta Damaris, the High Queen of Hael, her royal majesty, bid me deliver this to you."

Once she handed over a sealed envelope, she stood there with her hand out, slowly blinking.

Without a word of protest, Asa pulled an earring from his ear—a gold hoop with a ruby setting—and set it on her palm in payment for her delivery services. "Thank you for your efforts."

She thrust the metal post through her ear, piercing it in front of us, then walked off slurping her coffee.

Shoving my thumb beneath the flap, I held my breath as I broke the seal. Stomach churning, I read aloud to Asa, *"Circumstances prevent me from meeting at our arranged time."*

After giving me a moment to continue, then realizing I was done, he reached for the paper. "That's it?"

"That's it." I slumped on my weary bones. "We're safe."

"Until we're not." He turned the paper over, but there was only the one line. "Still, a reprieve is a reprieve."

Another hour passed, during which I tore the note into tiny pieces as my anxiety ratcheted higher, and acid rose up the back of my throat.

"This might be a trap." I hated to admit it. "Maybe Clay put her on the phone under duress."

Any number of agents loyal to the director could be closing in on us, tightening the net to catch us.

Fear stroked icy fingers down my spine as it hit me, *really* hit me, how much trouble we could be in. The anticipation soured my stomach, and I began playing and replaying that brief phone call in my mind.

"I smell burnt sugar." Asa flared his nostrils, straightening to his full height. "And…mold?"

"We're standing next to the restroom reno." I'd noticed it our last time here, but I hadn't thought much of it until we posted up beside it. "And there's a Cinnabon around here too. Maybe more than one."

Hope, as always, ached too much to hold on to. Doubt was easier. It hurt less.

Absolute silence stuffed my ears, deafening me, as a white flicker caught my eye.

For a second, I thought it was a piece of trash volleyed in an updraft, but it was moving too fast.

And heading this way.

Right.

At.

Me.

"Rue."

A tiny moth smacked into my throat, choking me, and my tears transformed the terminal into watercolors.

"Colby." I cupped her with my hand to protect her like I wish I had done sooner. "Are you okay?"

"Yeah." She trembled against me until Asa bundled her in her blanket. "I am now."

"How did you get here?" I scanned the milling crowd of travelers but saw nothing amiss. "Is Clay…?"

"It's a long story." She burrowed deep into her blanket, until only her antennae were visible. "Can we get out of here first?"

"Did you come alone?" I hated to push her, but we had to know. "Or should we expect company?"

"I came all by myself."

"Well, that's terrifying." I held her as tight as I dared, tucking the blanket across my chest. "Asa?"

"I'll tell the agents to stand down," he said, stepping away to place the call.

After he returned, we exited the airport and waited for Fergal to loop around and pick us up at the curb. Arden was as anxious as we had been after the long wait, but she dialed back her enthusiasm.

Because, like most everyone else, Fergal didn't know about Colby beyond the fact she was my familiar.

For better or worse, that was about to change. To prevent this from happening again, it *had* to change.

"I was so scared," Colby whispered between my fingers. "It was dark and the director was there and…"

"Shh." I kissed the top of her fuzzy head, despite her funky smell. "I've got you." I held her close. "You're safe."

"Your familiar can talk." Fergal held my gaze in the rearview mirror. "That's…unique."

"This is Colby." I lifted her so he could see her better. "She's my daughter."

"Your…" he twisted in his seat with a curious stare aimed right at Asa, "…daughter?"

"Yes." Asa stroked her fuzzy back, pride and love marbling his features.

Colby bumped up to cat size, flung herself at Asa, and cuddled into his chest.

"And she's your familiar?" Fergal dropped his gaze when he noticed Asa watching him. "That's…"

"Unique?" Arden supplied with a grin as she turned to see Colby for herself. "Going forward, you should know that if you tell anyone about her, you'll cease to exist." A hardness entered her expression that both warmed and chilled me at once. "I like you, but Colby is family. Hurt her, and you're going down."

With that, Colby flitted to give Arden a quick hug. She waved shyly at Fergal then zoomed back into my arms where she drooped against me, exhausted. I wished we had time for her to recover, but there was none to spare. As soon as the Mayhews tumbled into the cargo area, Fergal pulled out into traffic.

"Look who's back." Marita ruffled Colby's fluff, and Derry tweaked her proboscis. "I'm glad you're okay."

"Thanks." The fuzz on her cheeks lifted in a blush. "I'm glad to be back."

"I hate to do it, sweetie," I cut into their greetings, "but I need to ask you some more questions."

"I know." She fisted her hands in my shirt. "It's fine." She held on tight. "I'll tell you what I know."

"Begin whenever you're ready." Asa picked a green speck off her antennae. "Take your time."

Asa couldn't stop touching her. I couldn't blame him. I wasn't sure I believed she was here.

Safe.

She was *safe*.

Yet her escape felt too easy. Harrowing, yes. But I couldn't see Clay not telling the director about her.

A thousand questions perched on the tip of my tongue, but I clenched my jaw, giving her a moment.

"Clay and I were on our way to you. It was after your meeting with Calixta." Her antennae grew taut. "I was on my way into his pocket when he got a phone call. I couldn't hear who it was, I was already in the insulated part, but I felt when he..." She flexed her hands, burying her face in my shirt. "He stopped being Clay."

The spell on the inside of his jacket pocket was meant to insulate little moth ears from hearing adult conversations. For the first time since I made that modification to Clay's wardrobe, I regretted it.

"I climbed out." She eased up enough to look up at me. "I saw his face, and I knew it was bad." She swallowed. "I tried to get through to him, but he wasn't..." Her expression crumpled. "He wasn't Clay anymore." Her antennae drooped down her back. "He didn't know what to do with me, so he put me in a jar."

"He put you in a jar?"

"There were air holes," she rushed to add, "and food and water."

"Wait." I tried to make that fit what I knew of his blackouts. "He did that on his own?"

"Yeah." She tucked her wings in tighter against her back. "He was very careful not to hurt me."

Leaning forward, Asa appeared to steel his resolve. "Did he show you to the director?"

"No." A shudder rippled through her. "He kept me hidden from him." She rubbed her hands together. "I might have also started refer-ring to him as Big Nose Baron to make him less scary."

"From Mystic Seas," Asa explained for my benefit, his lips curving.

Big Nose Baron was nicer than any of the names I would have called him.

"Clay kept you in his pocket?" I wanted to be sure I got the whole picture. "Did you see the director at any point?"

"The jar was tall enough I could fly to the top and hear what they were saying. Sometimes. It depended on how Clay was sitting. That was how I knew about Charlotte. Oh. Clay mentioned another safe house in Dallas, if that helps."

"I'll text Isiforos," I decided. "He can shift the Kellies' focus toward Dallas in case the director decides to run there next."

Now that I thought about it, that was a lot of movement for him. He preferred to find a secure location and hunker down. Maybe Clay had convinced him that keeping on the move was the best way not to get caught? Hard to say without more information, but it was interesting that he chose Charlotte when Luca had too.

"The Kellies?" Colby's eyes brightened. "They're alive?"

"They are, and they're in Boston. They've taken over the setup you and Clay were working on."

"Good deal." She puffed up her fluff. "That means I can get back to the important stuff."

I got the feeling *the important stuff* was, to Colby, locating Clay. I couldn't say I blamed her.

"The Kellies are more than capable of resuming regular Bureau operations." Fergal turned back to the front. "As Colby said, we can focus on the more critical matters."

Clay.

The director.

Luca.

Calixta.

Aedan.

The list went on and on.

The easy way Fergal accepted Colby as a member of the team, affording her the respect she had earned, made me like him even more.

Asa, still focused on Colby, hadn't finished questioning her yet. "How did you get here?"

"Better yet—" I thought back on what she had told us so far, "— how did you get out of the jar?"

"Oh." She shuffled her legs and ducked her head. "I told Robo-Clay I had to pee."

"He bought that?" I gawked at her or maybe at the nickname. "He let you out?"

"He released me in the bathroom," she confirmed in a quiet voice. "He stayed with me, though."

"Is it possible...?" Asa voiced what I couldn't wrap my head around. "Could he have remembered her?"

"It would be a first," I admitted. "He can identify people in that mindset. It's not like he forgets everyone he knows. He might even be aware of how he *should* feel, but he doesn't experience it. It's not emotion, it's background noise, and since he doesn't recall his actions later, we'll never know for sure."

The catch in my voice told them I had never broken through the dissociation, no matter how hard I tried, and that never lost its sting. But, if anyone could do it, it would be Colby.

Invested in the story, Arden wedged her shoulders between the front seats. "Did you escape through the vent?"

"He taped them shut. Blocked the crack under the door too." Her proboscis twitched. "I used the drain."

"In the *tub*?" A million ways that could have gone wrong strobed through my head. "He could have turned on the hot water." I couldn't stop the nightmares from spawning. "He could have dumped a gallon of bleach on your head or—"

"I had to risk it." Her head came up, her eyes bright. "I had to get out of there."

"She's right." Asa smoothed his knuckles across my jaw. "Whatever his reasons, Clay didn't hurt her. The director would have, and Clay couldn't have stopped him. Even if he wanted to, he'd have had no choice."

"I know." I crushed my eyes closed. "I know." I rocked Colby, soothing us both. "I'm sorry."

"I did what you would have done." She didn't budge. "That's how I knew it was the right thing to do."

Goddess bless, what a mess.

The last thing anyone should ask themselves was *What Would Rue Do?* I wasn't a role model. How could no one tell I was utterly clueless? That I was flying through life by the seat of my pants? That I was a bad idea waiting to happen?

"You were brave." Asa stepped in when I couldn't get my mouth to cooperate. "We're very proud."

Fluffing herself up, she glided down onto the seat between us. "You haven't even heard the best part."

Half joking, I managed to mumble, "I'm afraid to ask."

"We were at a hotel, right? The drain kept going and going, and I was scared I would never get out. So I waited *forever* then climbed back up into the tub. Clay and the Big Nose Baron had already left, so I was able to use the room phone. I called the airport and checked flight times. The connection was horrible, but I guess no one really uses them anymore. Anyway. Then I called you and gave you my arrival time."

That part tripped me up enough to interrupt. "How...?"

"Oh. I could hear airplanes, so I knew the hotel was close to the airport. I crawled under the room's door into the hall and waited to catch a ride down to the lobby. *Then* I had to wait until someone stepped out to trigger the automatic door. And *then* I waited for the shuttle and got on. I got off at the airport, found my flight, and waited in the terminal until it was time to board. There was a mechanical delay, but otherwise—" her fuzz managed to reach new heights, "—I had a prime seat on the ceiling in first class. I even watched an upside down movie." Her antennae rose higher. "So, when do we get Clay back?"

"You said he was coming to Charlotte?" I got my jaw working, my brain too. "Any idea from where?"

Had Luca been here first? Or had the director? What did it mean that they were both here now?

"Manchester, New Hampshire." A troubled expression settled across her features. "Did you fly in too?"

"We were already here." I hadn't let it bother me, the coincidence factor, but now we had to consider it. I must have sensed Colby. Somehow. As glad as I was for that nudge, I had to question if that meant the bindings on me were fraying. "Luca shifted her operation to Charlotte. The death toll is rising, so we came to speak to the locals and reassure them the Bureau has everything under control."

Too bad that last part wasn't *quite* true.

"Do you have any idea how long ago you overheard the conversation between Clay and the director?"

"Good point, Asa." A timeline could answer a lot of questions if we could nail down one. "Colby?"

"I'm not sure." She rubbed her hands together. "I really did hide in that drain *forever*."

A kid's idea of forever wasn't the same as an adult's perception of time, but what we had so far made it a crapshoot which came first. The director. Or Luca.

"No worries," I assured her. "We'll figure it out."

"About that." A devious glint made her eyes gleam. "The timing doesn't matter."

The soft laugh from Arden proved she had learned just how resourceful our girl was in a pinch.

Asa, whose lips began contemplating a smile, asked, "Why not?"

"I cast a spell on his wig." Pride ruffled her wings. "Now we can track him."

Robo-Clay, as she called him, wasn't vain. He was practical. He would wear the wig until it got dirty or he got itchy. Then he would tear it off and toss it. That meant we had a small window of opportunity to benefit from Colby's wits before we found an expensive ball of hair in a trash can.

But to track Colby's magic, I would need Dad's help.

That meant, ready or not, I had to introduce him to Colby.

CHAPTER TEN

*N*o one tells you how awkward it gets when you introduce the daughter of your heart to your father.

Especially when one qualifies as a delicacy for the other. I was just glad Derry carried a packet of wet wipes for cleaning Marita's fingers when she ate sticky foods. I used one to scrub down Colby so she made a proper first impression.

To make their first meeting as low stress as possible, I invited my parents to join us at Freedom Park. With ninety-eight acres to choose from, we had plenty of privacy. And space. In case anything went wrong. I also had the Mayhews patrolling to watch our backs.

As much as I wanted to believe Dad wouldn't hurt Colby, I wasn't willing to take the chance. Both our lives were at stake if he acted before thinking. But, assuming we made it past the initial *hellos*, we ought to be golden. I had to drive home the whole *kill her and you kill me* thing. Fast.

Not that I envisioned Dad as a ravening beast (anymore), but this was Colby. Fear for her safety, worse so soon after being reunited, overrode any rapport I had built with Dad.

"You know you can tell us anything." Mom stood with her arm

looped through Dad's, either out of habit or to restrain him. I wasn't sure which. "What's got you so worked up, sweetheart?"

"I want to introduce you to my daughter."

The air thinned until it hurt to breathe.

Oh. No. It didn't.

Oops.

I forgot to inhale.

"Your *daughter*?" Mom dropped Dad's arm like a bad habit, clasping her hands at her chest. "Where is she?"

"Dad." I couldn't read his expression. "I'm going to need your word that you won't harm her."

A flicker of hurt shadowed his expression. "You think I would harm my own grandchild?"

"It's complicated." Asa stood behind me with his hand on my shoulder. "You'll see after you've met her."

"I assume this child is his?" Dad growled the accusation. "Well?" He glared at Asa. "Is she?"

"Yes." A smile played on his mouth that I wanted to kiss right off him. "She is."

Reaching into his jacket pocket, he withdrew Colby with a gentleness that warmed my heart.

"That is a moth." Dad blinked at her and then me. "And…" A breath punched from his lungs. "A *loinnir*."

"Yes." I angled myself in front of Asa, between Dad and Colby. "She is."

"She's *adorable*." Mom rushed over, a streamer of blue light in her wake. "Hi, baby."

"I'm *not* a baby." Colby kept her tone polite, but her eyes cut to me. "I'm…*me*."

"She can talk." Dad blinked again. "She's sentient."

"She's our granddaughter. Of course she can talk. I bet she's a genius. She looks brilliant, doesn't she? Look at that face!" Mom almost bounced in place. "Can I hold her? *Please?*"

"Rue." Dad drew my attention when the question lingered too long. "I vow on Howl's life not to hurt Colby today or ever. I understand why you're afraid for her, but her life is tied to yours, isn't it? How could you believe I would hurt you?"

"Habit." I rubbed my nape. "Colby *is* brilliant, by the way. You don't have to babytalk her or talk over her."

So far, she had been tolerant, but her age and her mental acuity were sore spots for her.

"I'm sorry, sweetie." Mom held out her arm, turning her palm upright. "I'm so excited to meet you."

After a brief pause, Colby glided over and landed, allowing Mom to look her fill.

Heart clogging my throat, I rasped, "Size up, just in case."

In a blink, she had bumped up to cat-sized, which let me relax a fraction.

Moths were so easy to crush, to wound, even on accident. Her next size up gave her more heft and substance, making it easier for those who didn't know her well to handle her safely.

"You control your size?" Dad's eyes brightened as Mom shifted her grip. "Remarkable."

"You don't know the half of it." I walked over and kissed Colby's head, unable to stop myself. "She's the best thing that's ever happened to me." I met his eyes, then Mom's. "She saved me. From the director and…from myself."

"You saved me too," Colby reminded me. "I wouldn't be here if you hadn't protected me."

When my parents prompted me for details with matching stares, I shook my head and mouthed *later*.

There was no reason not to tell them her story now, but I wouldn't force Colby to relive that day again.

"She cast a tracking spell on Clay." I was so proud I could pop. "Can you help us activate it?"

"I thought you would do it." She glanced between Dad and me then fell silent. "You feel weird."

Had she not been so stressed, she would have noticed the dissonance sooner.

"I was forced to bind her magic," Dad admitted. "The Hunk was attempting to merge with her."

"Are you okay?" She ditched Mom, zooming at me, knocking me back a step. "You can have my magic, if you need it."

"I'm fine—" I ruffled her antennae, "—but thank you for the offer."

"We would be happy to help." Mom beamed at us. "Anything for that cutie pie."

Dad, who was less versed in kids, softened his voice. "You thought of that all by yourself?"

"I've seen Rue do it a billion times." Colby fluffed with indignation. "I'm not a baby. I'm ten years old."

"Forgive me." Dad inclined his head. "What other ten-year-old would have thought of it?"

"He's impressed," Mom translated for him. "He's also patting himself on the back for having such a resourceful granddaughter." She snorted. "He's proud of you. That's all."

"Oh." Colby quit bristling. "Thanks." She cuddled into me. "Rue taught me everything I know." Her brow wrinkled. "Except computer stuff. And phones. And tablets. And—"

"We get it," I grumped. "You're the brains of the operation."

"You taught me witchy stuff," she consoled me. "And how to channel my powers."

"Yeah, yeah." I rolled my eyes. "Stop while you're ahead, smarty fuzz butt."

Her laughter was bright and filled me with gratitude that she was here for me to hear it.

"I mean it." Her amusement frayed along its edges. "I couldn't save myself…last time." She swallowed hard. "Thanks to you, and what you've taught me, I was able to escape."

"You did that on your own." I stroked her silky head. "I can take credit for the spell, but you were the one who thought to cast it. You kept calm, used that big brain of yours, and saved yourself."

"Oh." Her antennae vibrated. "That reminds me. I need to use your computer. Fast. I have to log into my account and wipe my laptop.

Clay brought it with us. He didn't mess with it that I saw, but it's dangerous for him to have access to it since he knows most of my passwords."

"I'll dig around in my bag." A tingle spread through my cheeks. "I'm sixty-eight percent sure I brought it."

"That sounds like a made-up number." Colby groaned. "I'll use Asa's if yours got lost." She sighed. "Again."

"We should begin." Asa rubbed her back, over her grimy wings. "We don't know how long we've got."

"Will the spell still work?" She peered up at Dad. "I was counting on Rue and the familiar bond to activate it."

"We're family." Dad stepped forward. "We can sense each other's power signatures, if we know them."

Without a hint of fear, she flew onto his shoulder and settled in. "You can read me. I don't mind."

The awkwardness with which he touched me was absent as he settled a gentle hand on her back.

Clenching abdominal muscles aside, I trusted she was safe with him.

A low bark drew my attention to Marita, who tilted her head in question. I shot her a thumbs-up, and she retreated with Derry beside her. Probably eager to shift and join the conversation now that we were all playing nice together.

"The path is faint," Dad said after a moment, "but she's powerful."

"Does that mean you can do it?" Her antennae perked. "We really, *really* need to get Clay back."

A text chimed at my hip, and I pulled out my phone to find an update from Isiforos on Luca.

>>*We have five new poisonings.*

>*Where?*

>*Give me directions, and I'll head that way.*

>>*In Dallas.*

>>*The cleaners confirmed king killer is the culprit.*

>*Boston, Charlotte, Dallas.*

>*Luca is flying with this stuff. She has to be. Why else go that route?*

>>*We don't know for certain she's handling it personally.*

The reminder was one that usually fell to Clay, but I didn't let myself dwell.

>*Tell the Kellies to double down on locating any properties the director owns and cut his funding ASAP.*

I had already begun my campaign of *everything is A-okay at Black Hat*, but this would prove me a liar as another city fell prey to Luca. We needed a win. The Kellies were recovering from their ordeal, yes, but we needed their skill and personal knowledge of the director now more than ever.

>>*Will do.*

Once I updated everyone, we all turned to Dad, waiting to see what he had gleaned from Colby's spell.

"Clay isn't in Charlotte." He let his eyes go unfocused as he traced the threads of power. "He's out west."

"Out west," I repeated. "As in, the same direction Luca just moved her operation?"

Chicken or the egg. Which came first? Had the director chosen Dallas? Or had she?

"I can't be certain without a map and crystal to dowse for Clay." He shook his head. "He's too far away."

"This can't be a coincidence." Asa thinned his lips. "Could Luca be tracking the director?"

"This whole hot mess is at the heart of her revenge plot," Marita said, joining us, "so I would say *yes*."

"They were intimate for decades." I fought not to gag on those words. "She could have a lock of his hair, nail clippings, or any number of other personal items collected over the years."

"Or—" Derry butted in, "—maybe *he* is tracking *her*. She's backed him into a corner. He has nothing left to lose. Either he spends the rest of his life on the run, or he faces her."

"The way he left things," Asa agreed, "he would have been a fool to break off contact with Luca without taking precautions."

"He would have taken every precaution," Dad agreed. "He doesn't let enemies go without insurance."

Thanks to Luca, he was exposed in a way he hadn't been since before he built the compound to shield him from the consequences of his actions. *If* he was hunting her, and that was a big if, it must have sunk in that he would never be safe as long as she was alive.

By taking everything away from him, she had struck a nerve. And, in the process, might have finally awoken a taste for vengeance within him to match hers.

"I'm telling you." Marita spread her hands. "Woman scorned."

"She cost him everything. His home, his legacy, his reputation. He has nothing left to lose." Dad tucked a loose curl behind his ear, pitching his lot in with Derry. "If he's set his sights on her, if he intends for her to pay for what she's done, it will make him more dangerous than ever."

"On the bright side," I added to avoid choosing sides, "if Luca is hunting the director too, we might all catch up to one another."

"In Texas," Marita clarified. "Big state, Texas."

"Lots of barbecue." Derry nodded. "Tons of ribs. Pulled pork. Burnt ends. Chicken."

"We should bring white sauce for the chicken." Marita pursed her lips. "The *original* white sauce."

The mayo-based sauce was invented in Decatur, Alabama, by Big Bob Gibson, and the Mayhews were addicted to his brand.

"We're getting sidetracked." They were also making me hungry. "Dad?"

"Clay is heading west." He spread his hands. "Without proper tools, that's the best I can do."

With fresh resolve, Colby sailed over to perch on Asa's shoulder. "Then let's get you the tools."

"We can print a map." Asa angled toward me. "Do you have a crystal your dad can use?"

About to confess how I stomped mine in the sand in a fit of pique, Dad saved me by saying, "I have one."

"Then let's go to the nearest office supply store. I can pull up a map on your computer while I'm remote wiping my laptop, pair it with their printer, and make a few copies." Colby caught me watching her and frowned. "What?"

The ache in my chest unspooled until I could breathe again. "It's nice having you back."

Asa, Colby, and I returned to the SUV, where Colby gave him directions to the nearest suitable location.

As per usual, Dad preferred flight to modern conveyances, and tracked us from the sky.

The remote print job took only a minute or two, and I rushed in to pay for the copies.

By the time I reached the SUV, I had collected four medium rocks and used them to secure the printout to the hood of the vehicle. Dad landed with the leather thong of his pendant wrapped around his hand.

When I glanced back, I found Mom holding Colby on her palm, cooing at her, and falling into babytalk. There was an infinite amount of patience on Colby's face, but when she cut her eyes toward me, I experienced a phantom twinge in the vicinity of my wallet. Something told me this was going to cost me later.

"They're in a car or on a plane," Dad informed us a few minutes later. "They're moving fast."

The most likely scenario was Clay playing chauffeur in a rental, allowing the director to travel incognito. He was bland enough, but it was hard to miss Clay. Even without his vast array of wigs, he was a big man who took up a lot of space, which was in short supply on a plane. Passengers who required entire rows for their broad shoulders tended to stick out in people's minds.

Whether he was the cat or the mouse in this scenario, he wouldn't want word of his movements leaked.

Itching to get moving, I pressed for more details. "Where are they now?"

"According to the map, in the vicinity of Shreveport, Louisiana."

Less than a minute later, Colby had opened a new tab and pulled up maps.

"That tracks," she confirmed. "It's along I-20 West. That's the quickest route to Dallas from Charlotte."

With all the other players on the move, we had to roll out or risk missing out soon.

CHAPTER ELEVEN

The Golem

MASTER IS NOT HAPPY.

The golem is not sure…

…why.

But.

He is not happy. Either.

The moth girl. Is gone. Down the drain.

The golem shouldn't. Care.

Doesn't care.

Can't.

But that name—*Clay*—echoes. In his head. Sometimes. Like someone calling out. For him. But he can't answer.

The phone rings. In the car that smells like fresh leather. Master tells him to answer.

So.

He.

Does.

Whatever Master says.

He.

Does.

"We found her, sir." A man with a deep voice booms. "She's moving her operation to Oak Lawn."

"Are you certain?"

Master does not believe him. The golem can tell.

"We have witches spread throughout the city," the man assures Master. "They're using the samples you gave me to fuel the tracking spell."

"All right." Master sounds pleased with this turn of events. "I'll be there soon."

He snaps his fingers, and the golem ends the call.

"She thinks she's hunting me." He smiles to himself. "She doesn't realize I'm hunting her."

"Yes, Master."

"Your aura is dimmer than before," he says, his eyes cunning in the rearview mirror.

"I will recharge when we arrive at our destination."

"Hmm." Master continues to stare at him. "Curious."

The golem doesn't ask.

Master will tell him. What he needs to know.

But the master doesn't. Need to know. About the moth.

Or how the golem…

…let her go.

CHAPTER TWELVE

*W*e beat the director to Dallas. Dad confirmed it after we regrouped at a hotel to eat and rest. And wait.

I didn't want to do any of those things, but my body had other ideas. I was punier without magic giving a boost to every aspect of my life. I hadn't realized how much ambient magic I channeled until I had none.

Fergal, who was eager to stretch his legs after spending so much time cooped up in the SUV to hide from the sun, handled the meeting with the local police chief, an eagle shifter who wished to discuss strategy for eradicating the threat Luca posed to his city.

Arden, to no one's surprise, tagged along after him. I was starting to think of her as his shadow.

That meant I got to sleep four hours, the maximum I allowed myself, and eat greasy fries and burgers.

The food scene in Dallas was incredible, but I still didn't feel right enjoying it without Clay, so I stuck to fast food restaurants with three star Yelp ratings as penance.

As I exited the shower, tugging on clothes as I went, Asa updated me. "Moran texted."

For that to happen, she had returned to the farm to use her phone, working against the time difference.

I hadn't heard from Carver since I sent him to Hael, and I didn't expect contact until after he returned unless it all went spectacularly wrong. Which, given Moran had crossed realms for reception, might have rendered that point moot. "How bad is it?"

"The skirmishes have escalated, and not by our choice." His lips drew into a flat line. "It seems our strategic strikes have emboldened the people to join in."

"We knew it was a risk." I bit my tongue when my response came out sounding dismissive in the face of what he had risked for me. Namely the lives of his centuria. "What can we do? How do we help?"

"Moran suggests we hold steady." He caught himself twisting an earring in a nervous habit and lowered his arm. "She's leveraging her status as primipilus to fold any dissenters they encounter into smaller groups headed by centurions."

"Are these, by any chance, the pro-Asa faction Carver informed us of?"

"Yes." His expression pinched. "That's why Moran can direct their efforts. They're aware of who she is to me. They believe she's creating chaos to unseat Calixta, and they're willing to follow her orders."

"The harder I try to save everyone, the more people suffer for it."

There must be a line, right? One I wouldn't be willing to cross for family. But I had yet to hit that limit.

I wasn't a good person. I never claimed to be. But I was better than I had been.

Maybe accepting that was as enlightened as I got. That and embracing the fault for the choices I made.

"The threat Luca poses goes far beyond Black Hat collateral. Her focus is on the larger paranormal community, and our response must also be on that scale." He came to me, gathering me against his chest. "The director, in addition to his value as a hostage, is a danger to anyone who crosses him. With Luca determined to flush him out of hiding, the body count will only climb higher if we don't stop them."

The director would have to pick the one woman with unlimited access to an incurable poison to spurn.

"Right now," Asa kept going, "Clay is our best chance at finding the director. There's no harm in pursuing a personal agenda when one path accomplishes two goals. If that leads us to Luca, or Luca to us, even better."

"What you didn't say was that if I had confessed to Calixta that I lost the director, if I had been willing to sacrifice Aedan too, I could have spared lives in Hael." I withdrew from the comfort I didn't deserve. "No matter how you spin it, I'm being selfish. People will die for my cousin, if they haven't already."

Is he worth it?

To me?

Yes.

Always.

But could I live with myself if I toppled the very monarchy meant to protect him during his tenure as prince? I had to cement Calixta's rule. She was the one I had leverage against. But it would cost lives to buy me time to find the director if Moran lost control even for a second, which was too much blame to place at her feet. She was from Hael. These were her people. And I was using them to advance my own agenda.

At the end of the day, I had enough black witch left in me to set fire to the world and watch it burn if it meant keeping my family safe. It wasn't right. It wasn't good. It wasn't fair. But it was true.

A knock on the door gave us a moment of warning before Dad strolled into our room.

"Clay is downtown." He clutched his crystal in his palm. "Near Hainsworth Distillery."

"We did an experiment." Colby, I noticed, sat on his shoulder. "Turns out Saint can dowse over a *tablet*."

Part of me noted that she had settled on calling him Saint, and that it seemed to please him.

"That's impressive," I admitted, forcing my mind back on task, "and also something I wish we had figured out sooner."

"Your mother has a strong affinity for dowsing." Dad maintained a rigid posture, as if he was afraid one wrong move would send Colby fluttering away from him. "That could be the reason why it's effective. Now our powers are linked by the familiar bond, and she could be boosting my proficiency in that area."

"I'll have to try it sometime." I did my best not to show how frustrated I was by my own lack of ability, but I felt like I was working this case with one hand tied behind my back. This experience had made it clear to me how often I used brute magical force to solve my problems. Maybe I should work on that. Using my brain instead of my magical brawn. "Are Marita and Derry out there?"

"They'll return soon." He glanced over his shoulder as Mom entered the room. "They went to get food."

"No surprise there." I soaked up the sight of my parents crowding Colby. "Those two could eat the state of Texas out of beef. Or pork. Or chicken. Or really anything digestible."

Probably a few things that weren't too.

"Meg ate her burgers so rare, I swear they still mooed." Mom shuddered. "I prefer my cow well done."

"Sometimes Clay makes me eat rare at fancy restaurants so I don't embarrass him in front of the chef."

"I've never understood that." Mom clucked her tongue. "Don't they know you'll enjoy what you're eating more if it's done to your satisfaction?"

"According to Clay, no."

About five minutes later, Derry and Marita walked in with food… and Arden.

"You're back." I glanced past her shoulder. "Where's Fergal?"

"He's gone hunting." Arden didn't bat an eye. "He said we should go ahead. He'll catch up in thirty."

The blood, guts, and heartache of the last several days had worked wonders on what I originally worried might grow into an infatuation on Arden's side. The hurt of losing Aedan, the wonder of this new world, and gaining a vampire mentor had left me concerned she might see Fergal as a Band-Aid for her broken heart.

Her quick dismissal of him hunting—a fellow human no less—stirred those worries again.

She was acclimating too quickly to her new reality. Maybe it was buried trauma from the Silver Stag copycat kidnapping her, scarring her. Maybe it was shock numbing her. Or determination fueling her.

Call it what you like, there was a therapist appointment with her name on it in the near future. With someone versed in counseling humans with paranormal affiliations, someone aware of the threats that came along with those relationships. To thrive in this world, she first had to be able to survive in it.

With Fergal absent, Asa climbed behind the wheel, and I claimed my seat beside him.

The Mayhews curled together in the cargo area, watching video clips on their phones.

Arden and Colby hung out on the bench, next to the Clay-shaped hole in our lives while Dad flew.

The trip was a short one, which did nothing to calm my nerves at the possibility of seeing Clay soon.

"A distillery." I hummed low in my throat. "I wonder if Luca is shifting her focus."

"We're tracking Clay," Asa reminded me, but he looked thoughtful. "Not Luca."

The gentle rebuke pulled me up short, but it made so much sense for this to come back to her.

"She could add it to the mash," Arden ventured then shrugged when I raised my eyebrows. "I have an aunt who dabbles."

Plenty of folks in Samford tinkered with moonshine, but craft beer? "What goes in it?"

"Corn, sorghum, malted barley, rye, or wheat." She scrunched up her face. "I think."

"Luca would have better luck skipping the fermentation process and mixing the king killer into what's already on tap," Marita reasoned. "They could kill a lot more people with one batch of poison-laced beer than they could with their current method."

"We're here for Clay," Asa warned again before we got too invested in the idea.

"You're right, you're right. I'm sorry. I shouldn't have fanned the flames of speculation."

The slight possibility we might be on to something nudged me to text Isiforos, just to be sure.

>*Any indication Luca is heading to Dallas?*

>>*The Kellies haven't isolated any footage that pings on facial recognition software.*

>>*If she's on the move, we're not seeing it.*

That didn't mean much when magic was involved, but he could only do so much.

>*Let me know if that changes.*

"Colby?" I mined the recesses of my memories. "You and Clay have a facial recognition program, right?"

"Yeah. Well. It's the Bureau's proprietary software." She stopped what she was doing to award me her full attention. "We've been tweaking it case by case to suit our needs."

"Can you grab the airport footage in Boston, Charlotte, and Dallas, and feed it through?"

"Sure thing." Her focus dipped back to the screen. "I'll see what I come up with."

"Let me know if I can help." Arden meshed her fingers, twisting them. "I'm not a pro like you, but I took a few computer classes in school."

"Clay and I always work better together." She angled the screen toward Arden. "Scooch in."

While the girls settled into their tasks, their collaboration giving me the warm and fuzzies every time, I tuned in to hear the plan. With me packing less firepower, we had to be smart about our approach.

The property itself was about an acre lot with five low-slung buildings. The nearest neighbor was about a mile away on either side. The trees would help muffle sound if things got heated, but the situation had the potential to go sideways fast. If that happened, the noise would be the least of our problems.

"Saint can handle aerial scouting." Derry's eyes brightened. "Marita and I will take the ground."

"Locating Clay and determining whether he's here alone or with the director is our top priority." I wiped my palms down my jeans. "We'll determine next steps after we know more."

"What about me?" Arden leaned forward, putting her face in mine. "I want to help."

"Put on your gloves." I locked down my jittery pulse, indicating for Asa to get out and wait on me. "Then get behind the wheel."

The pair of fingerless Tinkkit gloves Asa knitted her might allow Arden to turn her opponents' strength against them, but she was still human and oh so very fragile.

"Drive if I can." She climbed over the console. "Fight if I can't."

"Exactly." I slid my attention to Colby. "Don't let them get their hands on you."

She might have slipped away from Clay once, which still didn't jive with what I knew about him when he operated in that dead-eyed mode, but I wasn't risking her a second time.

The Mayhews exited the SUV and initiated their changes while Dad began the dowsing process over the tablet Colby had zoomed in to frame our area. Sure enough, the crystal indicated the building to our left.

"Let's do this." I rocked forward only to bump into Dad. "What?"

"You're not going." His jaw was granite. "If Father is in there, you're defenseless against him."

Asa parted his lips then snapped his mouth shut without bringing my magic—or lack thereof—into this.

"I'm not standing out here, providing a free mosquito dinner buffet."

Marita nudged my hand with her cold nose then jerked her head to indicate she and Derry were leaving.

"Be safe." I scratched behind her ears. "Do *not* engage."

Behind her, Derry chuffed in the next best thing to a promise from his wolf.

Once they padded off, Dad rolled his shoulders to shake out his wings. "Watch the girls."

Being relegated to guard duty sucked. Realizing Asa was essentially on guard duty for the guard on duty? Yeah. Not my finest moment.

Ten minutes later, Asa couldn't stop his eyes from crinkling. "You hate this."

"You'll have to define *this*." I kicked the nearest tire. "There's a lot to hate right now."

"You're used to being the one who solves everyone else's problems."

Power like mine altered a wielder's outlook. Especially with a black magic amplifier like the Hunk making all things possible.

"That's a charitable outlook on me." I almost laughed. "I'm used to being a hammer in search of a nail."

"But all the nails have turned into screws."

"Yes." A chuckle slipped through. "All the nails have turned into screws."

A bolt of white-hot agony shot down my spine, turning my legs to jelly, and my knees buckled on me.

"Rue." Asa gripped my arms to hold me upright. "What's—?"

Flames engulfed him, and Blay emerged with a snarl that raised the hairs down my nape.

"Witch," I panted, my limbs shaking.

"Blay smell." He eased me to a seated position with the SUV's wheel at my back. "Rue stay."

Before I could fight through the trembling to reach for him, he was gone, and I was left a sitting duck.

As it hit me how thoroughly screwed I was, how helpless I was in a magical firefight, a kernel of searing light ignited in the center of my chest. The rising tide of heat spread through me, burning like pure sunlight injected into my veins.

A pounding noise on the glass drew my attention to the windows, but I couldn't see through them.

I couldn't see *anything*.

"I don't understand." I clutched my head in my hands. "What's happening to me?"

Another round of knocks, this time in a familiar cadence, told me Colby was the one behind this.

As I turned my vision inward, I could sense a tendril of pure magic lighting me up from the inside out.

A loud pop rang out beside me, and metal screamed in my ears. I wobbled to my feet to find a grenade coated in spikes and putrid magic stuck in the door panel. I didn't think. I grabbed it, shredding my hand, and yanked until I fell back in the dirt on my back with the explosive skewering my palm.

"I'm sorry for this," Dad rasped from above my head, his wings stirring my hair.

Tipping back my head, I found him hovering with his hand outstretched toward me. I lifted my arm, let him rip out the grenade— along with copious amounts of my skin and blood—and vanish into the night sky. I sat there, crimson dripping through my fingers, lost in a haze where my eyes didn't quite focus.

An explosion rang out from the direction Dad had flown, and I hoped he had escaped the blast radius.

Ribbons of magic filled my vision in darting patterns as I tried to focus, and I understood with a gasp.

I was seeing magic. *Spells.* How was this possible? I had no access to my magic.

Colby.

She was reversing our familiar bond, sending me a torrent of her power for my use. Had I been less terrified as I realized that Dad's spell had frayed enough to allow it, I might have been more grateful.

A woman with dark-green hair slipped from behind the building, her gaze fixed on me.

"Luca was right." Her stride was confident as she ate up the ground between us. Meanwhile, I struggled with reacclimating to having magic that was both foreign and familiar. "She said you would come."

Goddess bless, what a mess.

We hadn't located Clay, as far as I knew. No word on the director either. Now Luca was here?

Had we actually been right? She was hunting the director? Okay. Fine. Then why had the director chosen a distillery manned with black witches under Luca's control? One had led the other here, but which?

"Who are you supposed to be?" I rubbed my eyes until my vision cleared enough to let me watch her stalk me. "Her lackeys all blend together after a while. Kind of hard to tell you apart, know what I mean?"

"I'm Fain." Her lips pinched until they turned white. "Hertzog witches aren't lackeys."

"And yet, here you are, doing Luca's bidding." I shrugged. "Kind of feels like what a lackey would do."

A blur of motion behind her kicked my heart into high gear, but as pale fingers closed around Fain's neck with punishing force, ripping her away from me, I recognized my savior.

"I apologize for my tardiness." Fergal wrestled her arms down by her sides. "I shouldn't have ordered an appetizer." He caught my look and chuckled. "Vampire humor."

"Okay, Fain." Now that I had backup, I shifted into interrogation mode. "Where's your boss?"

"Luca isn't my boss." She jerked up her chin. "What I do, I do for the cause."

A shudder tripped down my spine as I wondered if Moran was hearing—or giving—similar speeches.

"Oh, goddess." I leaned back against the SUV. "This should be good."

"Yes." Fergal's voice dripped with disdain. "Tell us about this righteous cause you serve."

"For too long, humans have held the upper hand. We have been forced to live in shadow while they—"

With a practiced twist of his wrists, Fergal snapped her neck, and she hit the dirt in a pile of limbs.

"There's no reasoning with the indoctrinated," he explained, then went rigid with vampire stillness.

"You killed her," Arden whispered through the window she must have cracked during the fight.

The otdrels we had killed fell easily into the category of *creature* rather than *human*.

Witches weren't human, black witches especially, but we sure looked like them.

Shuttering his expression, Fergal nodded once to me. He crept back into the shadows to hunt for more witches as Arden raised her window and slumped out of sight.

Just as I was crouching to search the body, a tall man burst from the shadows and aimed his wand at the SUV. I didn't think. I threw out my arm toward him, expecting an arc of deadly magic to shoot from my hand and strike him dead. But that trick belonged to the Hunk, not me, and nothing happened.

Except for me looking deranged for the split-second before old reflexes kicked in.

My one advantage was he had to touch the SUV to damage it. That suited me just fine. Since I had to make contact too, either through my wand or my hand, he was doing half the work for me by coming to me. All I had to do was make sure I tagged him before he contacted the metal.

As I drew on Colby's power, letting it burn through me as I fought for control of it, the witch in front of me lunged. I didn't see what happened next. Everything went loud and white and then black and silent.

CHAPTER THIRTEEN

*A*fter I regained consciousness, the only reason I didn't ground Colby for the rest of her life was because she had burned herself out helping me. I was still toying with the idea of banning her from Super Mystics during release week when Asa touched my arm.

Reflex tightened my fingers where I cradled an unconscious Colby across my blistered palms.

"She'll recover." He tucked her blanket around her. "She just needs rest."

Asa had carried me to the SUV and laid me across the bench seat after I blacked out mid-fight. I was sitting up now, mostly under my own power, but my brave little moth girl hadn't woken yet.

"How do you feel?" Dad stood beside Asa in the doorway. "You smell…"

"Crispy," Asa supplied. "Your hair is fried at the ends, and your nailbeds are scorched black."

"I taste barbecue every time I swallow." I had flakes on my tongue too. "Pretty sure the barbecue is me."

"Your familiar's magic is pure, but mine isn't. She was burning through it—through *you*—to help you." A thoughtful expression settled across Dad's features. "Perhaps that explains how she reached you. There's a possibility her ambient magic is eroding the bindings I placed on you."

If her power had been bashing against the block from her side, trying to get through, it could have done catastrophic damage to Dad's spell. Especially now that it had been breached once.

"That's…not great." I shut my eyes, hating how my earlier thoughts aligned with his. "That means the Hunk could break through at any moment." I hated to ask, but I didn't see another way. "Can you bind me again?"

"Not without undoing the original spell." Dad shook his head. "We can't risk it."

"The Hunk needs only seconds to devour you." Asa, for once, agreed with Dad. "It's too dangerous."

"We might not have a choice." I blinked away the sting of tears. "Eventually, I mean."

"We're clear." Marita opened the door opposite me. "No more witches on the ground."

"Luca," I gasped, tumbling into a coughing fit. "I forgot to tell you—"

"I relayed what I overheard the witch telling you." Fergal, who I had just noticed, was keeping a slight distance from the SUV, and from Arden. "Luca wasn't here. Neither was Clay, or the director."

"How is that possible?" I couldn't believe this was a total bust. "Could the tablet be the problem?"

I had never heard of a witch dowsing over one. Everyone I knew used paper maps. But I was old school.

"He was here." Dad left no room for argument. "The Mayhews didn't pick up his scent, so he didn't get out. He must have been surveilling the distillery from a parked vehicle on the access road we passed on the way in."

"That," Asa added, "could explain his quick exit when things got heated."

"If Clay saw what went down," I reasoned, "and that's why he left, he won't be back."

"He won't." Asa returned his focus to me. "But Luca might."

"We're already here." I bobbed a shoulder. "It won't hurt to hang around and see what shakes out."

"Might as well." Marita parked her naked butt beside me. "This group, man. They're whackadoodle."

"What do you mean?" I ignored the sounds of Derry shifting in a patch of darkness. "Who are they?"

"Word has spread about Luca and her rogue black witches." Fergal sounded closer. "This coven has no affiliation with Black Hat that the Kellies can find. That doesn't mean there isn't one, but it's buried deep."

Once other paras noticed what she was doing, we were bound to reach a point where newer supporters of her cause had heard it from a friend who heard it from a friend and so on. It was inevitable. Too many paras thought the way she did and would be glad to side with her to help bring forth a new world order.

"They're extremists," Derry panted, climbing to his feet. "They want paranormals to walk in the light, enslave humanity, become the gods of man, blah, blah, blah. The usual. I doubt Luca would have bothered allying with them, except they also own a local beer label. This one. Luca was coming here to finalize her plans and seal a bargain with them, or so they claimed during questioning, ceding control of Dallas to their coven after paras go mainstream."

"Goddess bless," I muttered, hating to be proven right. "Have they started production yet?"

"No." A coldness spread across Dad's features. "I interrogated them myself."

No one spoke for a moment, convincing me I was lucky to have missed out on the festivities.

"Do they have any idea when Luca is set to arrive?" I homed in on Dad. "If she's flying in?"

The hub idea was a solid one. It made the most sense, given the pattern of poisonings. But our best-case scenario was that we were playing follow the leader. Assuming Luca was tracking the director, and we were tracking Clay, who was with the director, that still left a lot of room for error.

"They're expecting her tomorrow night." He raised his gaze to mine, searching my face for, I think, condemnation of his methods. "She didn't share her travel arrangements."

This late in the game, she couldn't afford to trust sensitive information to anyone outside her original circle. These new witches were too motivated by their own desires—rather than hers—and she was smart enough to know any one of them would kill her and step into her shoes given half a chance.

"Okay." I hated I was relieved by the timetable. "Then we get a room and see what shakes out at dusk."

"Any survivors might warn her away." Asa stared at the bodies of the witches, tallying the dead. "If Nan, Luca's pet hacker," he clarified for the others' sakes, "retained access to the original Black Hat database, enough to force her way into the newest iteration, she can track our movements again."

"She would see if the cleaners were dispatched to the distillery," I muttered, "and cancel Luca's plans."

"That's the danger, yes."

"The old database." I had been receiving fewer tech updates in Clay's absence. Either the others thought I was more proficient than I was, or they lacked the patience to dumb down details for me. Probably the latter. "They're reviving it?"

Unsure what a database was, exactly, I had come too far to admit my total and complete ignorance now.

"Only as a temporary measure. They're going to copy all the files, do a data cleanse," Asa said, "then move servers. All agents will be required to set up new accounts and passwords to access it. Then the old database will be erased."

"I'm all for more security." Too bad it wouldn't do us any good any time soon. "What's next?"

"I'll dowse for Clay," Dad offered, stepping away, "try to figure out where he went from here."

"Makes sense to case the joint first." I turned my thoughts back to Clay. "See what he's up against."

"Hmm." Marita tilted her head. "You think there's a chance he missed the fireworks?"

"Maybe he got an eyeful of the Hertzog witches and decided to bide his time before making his move."

"From what Colby said, it sounds like the director is done hiding." Derry frowned. "Now that he knows Luca is responsible for his present circumstances, he won't stop until he eliminates her."

"I believe that's the point Rue is trying to make," Asa mused. "That, with the level of opposition, Clay would have left rather than engage if Luca wasn't present."

"Which he only could have known," I cut in, "if the director had means of tracking her."

The hope we had *just* missed him was a blow and a boon. As much as I wanted to set eyes on him, we had better odds of intercepting Luca if he hadn't witnessed our explosive encounter with the witches.

"Once he takes out Luca," Dad said, his words frosting over, "he'll eliminate Rue next."

"Try," Marita corrected him. "He'll *try* to eliminate her next."

"Then we'll kick his ass." Derry rolled a shoulder. "It's what friends do."

"Thanks, guys."

Hard as I fought to stay present, to bask in the glow of their affection, I couldn't fight the force dragging my lids down.

"CLAY IS HERE."

I groaned and turned away from the bright voice in my ear.

"Rue."

A familiar weight began trouncing me until my kidneys waved a white flag. Make that two white flags.

"I'm up," I wheezed, capturing Colby in a hug then dragging the sheet over our heads. "Have mercy."

"No mercy." She shoved against my chest. "Clay's *here*, Rue."

"Here?" Her earlier words replayed in my head, and I shot upright, earning a yelp from her. *"Here?"*

"Not *here* here, not the hotel." She yanked the cover down. "At the distillery."

The hotel we chose was three miles away, maybe four. We grabbed the nearest one after getting an all-clear from the cleaners, who agreed to keep their findings mum for twenty-four hours to give us time to intercept Clay. And the director. And, hopefully, Luca too.

"Why didn't anyone wake me?" I swung my legs over the side of the bed. "We need to go."

"I *did* wake you," she pointed out, zooming away. "Now, hurry up."

The door opened while I tugged on fresh clothes, and Asa passed me a glass of orange juice.

"Thanks." I gulped it down without tasting it. "Clay is really there?"

"According to your father, yes." He traded with me, forcing a breakfast sandwich into my hand. "He arrived ten minutes ago but hasn't moved since. He's either waiting for Luca in the car again or watching for her from a stationary position."

"Okay." I did a quick turn, making sure I had my wand, and decided I had everything I needed. "Let's go."

Asa and I rode the elevator down with Colby in my hair and found Marita and Derry waiting in the lobby.

Their eyes were bloodshot and their clothes filthy, an indication they had spent the day on patrol, but they vibrated with energy that prickled my skin.

Probably had something to do with how they both held a sixty-four-ounce cup of coffee in each hand.

"I can taste the color purple." Marita wet her lips. "It smells like chocolate."

"Um." I flicked a glance at Derry. "I see."

"She picked up someone else's coffee order. Turns out they put a little something in it along with cream and sugar. She's been high as a kite for the last ten minutes. If she wasn't sloshing with caffeine, it would have worn off by now." He smiled at her, love in his eyes. "She can also talk to bumblebees."

"Bzz-bzz," she confirmed, spinning away with her arms held out straight to her sides like a plane.

"What can we do to fix *that*?" I winced when she began using a broken tree limb as a stinger. She would be in a world of hurt if she fell with that stick down the back of her jeans. "How do we sober her up?"

"Here." Dad walked up behind me, scaring ten years off my life. "Get her to drink this."

"What is that?" Derry pushed off the wall. "A hangover cure?"

"Something like that." He passed off a small vial to Derry. "You can mix it in with her coffee, if you like."

"More coffee?" I worried my bottom lip with my teeth. "Are you sure that's wise?"

"Your mother formulated it." He watched Marita for a moment. "She's very familiar with warg biology."

For Dad to be carrying it around, Mom must have figured he would find a use for it. Probably after she discovered he had flown Marita and Derry in to help.

"That sounds like she made a lot of hangover cures for Meg back in the day." Derry snorted. "Here goes."

Without ceremony, he dumped the liquid into one of his cups then swirled it with his straw.

Gotta say, I was impressed when he required no further proof of Dad's intentions before going for it.

"Oh no. They gave me a caramel crunch Frappuccino by mistake," he called to Marita. "Do you want it?"

Still buzzing, she swooped in and took the cup, downing its contents in four large gulps.

"Send them ahead," Dad advised. "The shift will help burn off the lingering effects."

"Come on, Bumble." Derry led her toward the alley. "You heard the man."

Ticking off a mental roll call, I hit the next one. "Fergal?"

"Already in the SUV." Asa gestured toward the parking deck. "Arden has volunteered to protect Colby, so they will both remain with Fergal."

"Have we heard from Moran?"

"The centuria is holding their ground, but if Calixta decides to involve her military, it will get ugly."

"Okay." I pushed out an exhale. "We need to start brainstorming on how to fix that."

"Already ahead of you." Asa risked a smile. "I've enlisted Isiforos to help."

Since Isiforos's dad was our propaganda machine in Hael, thanks to his crafty side and ruthless merchandising streak, I didn't mind giving him more responsibility.

"Good." I checked my list twice, but there wasn't anything else actionable. "Let's go see what we see."

FOR THE SECOND DAY IN A ROW, I FOUND MYSELF STATIONED AT THE SUV while the others secured the distillery.

There was no sign of Clay when we arrived, a repeat of yesterday, and I didn't know what to make of it. Every time Dad dowsed, his crystal indicated Clay was here, but the wargs hadn't scented a hint of him.

Had the director cloaked him in magic to conceal him, they would have picked up on that instantly.

Unless…

Did the director have any pieces of the dark artifact Trinity and Markus Amherst had used to hide their black witch signatures? We suspected Luca used a shard from it to conceal her fae nature, which meant there was a chance the director had access to the pottery at some point as well.

"A black car is coming down the drive." Dad swooped over me. "There are two motorcycles behind it."

"This could be it." I relished the jump in my pulse. "Where can I get the best view?"

"Come with me." Dad hooked his hands under my armpits. "I'll take you to the storage building."

The roof he chose had a perfect view of the distillery, but it wasn't Luca who stepped out of the sleek car after it parked. It was Nan. Her hacker. She was joined by two other women I could tell were black witches thanks to them being upwind of us. They positively reeked of dark magic.

With a twist of his wrist, Dad cast a sound amplification spell that allowed us to listen in on their conversation, making me wish I could cast long distance. Or at all.

Pity party, table for one.

You know what? No. I was done with moping.

I was more than my magic. I had a brain. It was time I put it to use. Starting with how to get my hands on Nan and put *her* to good use.

"This place is a dump and a half," the escort on the right of Nan said. "How are they not killing people through poor hygiene alone?"

"Does hygiene apply to buildings?" the one on the left asked. "I thought that was a people thing."

"Botulism then." Righty tossed out the suggestion. "How about that?"

"The acidification during fermentation—"

"Enough," Nan snapped with a growl. "We're not health inspectors."

"How many people do you think she'll kill this time?" Righty was at it again. "Like fifty?"

"A hundred is a nice round number," Lefty countered. "The least she could do for my OCD is—"

The door leading into the front of the distillery swung open, and two men exited with their wands out.

Not good. Their unexpected appearance changed things. For the worse.

The main building had a ward spell. Crap. It had concealed these new witches' presence and who knows what else. It must have been old. Otherwise, the wargs would have mentioned it. As it was, I suspected they had mistaken the faint magic signature as foot traffic from yesterday's skirmish.

"You're not Luca," the taller one said in lieu of a greeting. "Who are you?"

"I'm Nan." She shouldered past her escorts. "I speak for Luca."

"The deal is off," the shorter man declared with a slice of his hand. "We deal with Luca or no one."

Bold stance, considering he hadn't confessed his coven was down half a dozen witches.

"I was hoping you'd say that." Lefty wet her lips. "Nan?"

"Hold." She stared at the taller man. "Where is Lakesha?"

"Dead." He rolled a shoulder, finally coming clean. "We were attacked last night."

"Why didn't you lead with that?" Nan growled, her hands balling into fists. "This operation has been compromised." She backed up, gaze darting to her surroundings. "We have no business here."

Temper getting the better of him, the shorter man stepped into her space. "Luca promised us—"

"Now?" Righty pleaded with a pout in her voice. "I'm hungry."

"Hungry?" The tall one bared his teeth. "We're not *food*."

Eerie cackles poured from the women flanking Nan as they lengthened their fingernails into talons.

"Make it quick." Nan heaved a sigh as they sprung. "I'll wait in the car."

Palming her phone, she fell into conversation as she marched back to her ride.

The update I suspected she was giving Luca fell outside the range of Dad's spell. All we got was surround sound for the carnage of the women feasting on the men's hearts. Their joy in the viciousness of it made my stomach twist to recall I had once been just like them.

"Do we follow Nan to listen in, or do we take the three of them out now?"

"The Mayhews are closing in on the women." He cut his eyes toward Nan. "Let her finish her update. That will buy us time before

Luca realizes Nan has been taken." He frowned. "Can Colby trace the call?"

"You're picking up on the lingo fast." I wondered how much of that was a result of osmosis from spending time around Colby. "She can do anything she sets her mind to and then some."

"She's lucky to have you." His eyes softened when they shifted onto me. "She loves you very much."

"Not half as much as I love her." I trawled my brain for the right words to make up for their introduction. "I'm sorry I didn't tell you sooner."

It felt like the right thing to say, even if I wasn't convinced it was true.

"She's your daughter." His lips twitched over the words. "I understand why you kept her a secret."

"It's a habit." I heard it for the cop-out it was. "And, okay, I didn't want you to eat her."

Before Mom factored into the equation, he had been dead set on fulfilling his animus vow. There hadn't been a reason to entrust him with Colby. Now that he planned on sticking around, I didn't have a choice.

If I wanted to reach a point where I had no secrets from the ones I loved, I had to start trusting them.

"You were right to protect her." His gaze went distant. "I wasn't myself when we first met."

Before we could dig into that, snarls rent the air, and the witches hissed, hunched over their kills.

"Wait here." Dad flexed his wings. "I'll intercept Nan."

Unsure what had tipped the Mayhews into motion before Dad gave the signal, I didn't hold him up when Nan was our best hope of finding Luca. But I didn't wait either. I hit the fire escape hanging over the side of the building and climbed down as fast as I dared, bumping into Blay when my feet hit the ground.

"Rue's dad told Blay to watch Rue." He folded his arms across his chest. "Rue not fight witches."

Now that I had accepted I had value, with or without magic, they had to get onboard with letting me take risks too. "Did you find Clay?"

Regret pinched his features as he presented me with a ball of hair that I shook out into a familiar wig.

"The director must have sensed the spell." I crumpled it in my fist. "This might prove Clay reported seeing us. As paranoid as the director is, he would have examined Clay." He would have noticed Colby's brightness countering his dark magic and known we were onto him. "Where did you find it?"

"Old car." He gestured toward the road. "Driver dead."

Chances were good the Hertzog coven had upped their security in response to last night's attack. Had they wondered at their good luck when the cleaners didn't record the mess they wiped away, allowing them to hope Luca wouldn't catch wind of it and pull out?

The witches must have spotted the driver, determined Luca wasn't with him, and killed him to avoid any potential interruptions. They hadn't had time to dump the body before Nan arrived, which was good for us. It explained why there had been no hint of Clay then or now and gave us a window for time of death.

"Could you tell if the driver was a black witch?"

"Blay found ID." He handed over a wallet. "Driver with Bureau."

Talk about the right hand of an organization not knowing what the left was doing. I had known, of course, that the director had his loyalists. How could he not? He knew his agents' secrets and was more than willing to wield them like blades against his people. But just how deep did this fissure run in the Bureau? That was what I had to figure out if I wanted control of the dangerous creatures in my employ.

"How did he die?"

"No heart." Blay shrugged. "Witch ate him."

Screams pierced the air as the wargs took down the witches, which meant Nan would have heard.

The crunching was hard to miss.

We had to close in on her or lose her, and she wouldn't be fool enough to get caught out in the open a second time.

"We should go help Dad." I begged with my eyes. "There are more witches waiting at the car."

How many more, I couldn't say, but someone had driven her.

"Rue stick with Blay?" His eyes held a wealth of doubt. "Rue be good?"

"I'll be good." I tugged on his arm. "Come on."

A minute later I was reminded why it was dangerous to send Dad after sensitive targets.

We found him standing over a male witch who must have been the driver I was just wondering about. He was dead. Really dead. He must have ticked Dad off to earn that level of evisceration.

Nan, her face purple, hung suspended midair, feet dangling above the driver's body.

Muttering to herself, she thrashed and fought. I thought I heard her curse Luca's name but wasn't sure.

"She's no good to us dead." I sprinted for Dad, grabbing his arm. "Set her down."

"She took a pill." A growl lodged in his chest. "She's dead anyway."

Now that shocked me. Nan wasn't the type to choose self-destruction. She was too sure of herself.

Maybe it was a ruse and she hoped the diversion would earn her a chance to escape? Hard to say. Either way, she was still fighting for her life. Which didn't fit her actions. She also looked *pissed*...but at herself? She coughed, gagging, her tongue rolling. Like she wanted to spit out the pill, but it wouldn't cooperate.

"Don't waste the time we have with her then." I caught her as Dad released her from his spell, wrangling her onto the ground away from the dead driver. "Talk fast." I gripped her shoulder. "Tell me something. Anything we can use against Luca."

Because I knew, I *knew*, the hatred burning in her eyes was for her former boss and not for me.

"What makes...you think I...will tell you...anything?"

"You're smart, and you're clever. You think highly of yourself, for good reason. Taking the easy way out? Just to protect Luca's secrets? Are you telling me it was *your* idea to pop that pill?"

Blood welled in the corners of her mouth. She parted her lips, but no sound escaped her.

"Luca bound you from spilling her secrets." I exhaled. "I bet she put that nasty compulsion on you too."

Nan hadn't chosen this end. It had been decided for her. That made more sense.

"Can you…save…me?"

"Depends." I tried to make her comfortable. "Was that king killer?"

She must have gotten her answer from my expression, and she shut her eyes.

"Nan." I shook her. "This is your one chance to pay Luca back."

The vow binding her might not allow for it, but I had to keep pushing while she was coherent.

"No."

"You're going to let her win?" A wave of disappointment crashed through me. "I thought you were made of sterner stuff than that."

"No…" She lifted her hand, aiming for the pocket on her jacket. "Take it."

Wary of reaching barehanded into enemy clothing, I hesitated, afraid I might slice my finger on a blade laced with king killer or worse. "What is it?"

A sigh gusted past her lips, and she fell still.

"She's dead," I called to Dad. "Do you have a knife on you?"

"An athame, yes." He drew it from a sheath at his ankle. "Be careful. It's sharp."

Concern gave way to curiosity as I sliced the pocket free then used the tips of my fingers to dump it out. I wasn't sure what the black stick that tumbled out was until after I picked it up, flipped open the top edge, and exposed a USB port.

"It's a thumb drive." I was shocked to remember the name for it. "Clay stores files like this."

Colby considered it old school, but I wasn't sure how she kept things stored in a cloud. The memory stick was tangible, and I understood what I could hold better than the theoretical. With technology anyway.

On my periphery, Blay was engulfed in flames that parted for Asa. "We need to get to a computer."

"This could be a virus." I was on a roll today, and Clay wasn't here to witness it. "It could infect us."

"You're right," Asa said, too many seconds past when it would have come out as a polite response.

"Colby will be so proud." About to pat myself on the back, I recalled she was in no shape to praise me.

"I've texted the cleaners." Asa checked his phone. "ETA is twenty minutes."

After shoving Clay's wig into my pocket, I strode toward the SUV. "Let's not be here when they arrive."

CHAPTER FOURTEEN

*T*he golem

PAIN BURST. IN THE GOLEM'S CHEEK WHEN. MASTER STRUCK HIM.

He didn't hit. Back.

He shouldn't want. To harm Master.

But his fist. Was tight. At his side.

His knuckles went...

Pop.

Pop.

Pop.

"Why didn't you tell me about the spell Rue put on your wig?"

Rue.

Rue, Rue, Rue.

The golem knew that. Name.

"I wasn't aware it had been cast." The words flowed from him. "I would have told you if I had known."

An odd sensation curled through his chest, rising up his throat, locking his jaw.

It was a…

…lie.

He was lying. To Master.

He *never* lied to. Master.

"We'll see about that." He tapped his cane three times on the tile. "Your ridiculous hairpiece is in the back of a car as we speak. The driver is running it all over Dallas then circling back to the distillery. If my granddaughter comes to fetch it, we'll know you have been compromised."

"Yes, Master."

"That jar." He slid his gaze behind the golem. "Why do you have it?"

"I caught a moth." The golem found he couldn't lie this time. "But it escaped."

"Peculiar." His fingers tightened on his cane. "You haven't been right since I paired you with my granddaughter. She's done something to you." His hard stare made the golem flinch. "You're old for one of your kind. It might be time to take you apart. Add some new clay. Work out the impurities. Then reanimate you."

"That would kill me."

The golem didn't know how he knew, but he understood the addition of more clay from the blessed pits where golems were molded would dilute the core of who he was until he wouldn't wonder where the moth girl went. If she was okay. If he should have kept her. Safe.

"That is exactly what I mean." Master turned, placed his hand on the door. "Don't leave this room."

"Yes, Master."

That was what the golem said. But for the first time.

He stared at the doorknob. Wondered what might happen.

If.

He.

Turned.

It.

CHAPTER FIFTEEN

*U*sing her blanket as a hood, Colby finished extracting the information on the thumb drive Nan gave me. I wasn't thrilled she was back at work the second her eyes opened, but the news about Clay hit her hard. She wasn't going to rest until she got her bestie back, so I might as well supervise. Otherwise, she would forget to eat or sleep. I had seen it happen a million times during Mystic Realms game-a-thons.

"There's a video." Her voice came out soft, tired. "Want me to cue it?"

We had retreated to the hotel to avoid the cleaners, crossing our fingers Nan had given us intel we could use to take down her boss and not a virus as a parting gift. I wanted to believe her fury had been genuine, but I wasn't confident enough to bet on it.

That was why we bought a laptop off a random teen in the lobby for twice what he paid for it.

"Yeah." I checked to make sure everyone had a clear view of the screen. "Let's see what we've got."

On screen, Nan typed a mile a minute, cutting brief glances at her laptop's camera.

"If you're watching this, whoever you are, I'm either dead—in which case, fuck you—or you robbed me. If you're a thief, your days are numbered. If you're not...then my mother was right and working for Luca was the death of me." She finished what she was doing and sat back in her chair. "Chances are you're either Rue Hollis or one of her minions." She shot a bird at the screen. "You're probably half the reason I'm dead." She exhaled. "But you're not wholly to blame."

"I have minions." I pursed my lips. "I like the sound of that."

"Your inner evil overlord is showing." Arden elbowed me. "Now hush."

"You've probably figured this out by now," Nan continued, "but I'll break it down in case you're behind."

"That was nice of you." Marita shot the laptop a thumbs-up. "Appreciate it."

"Hmm." Nan inclined her head. "Not sure where you are in the timeline." She sighed. "I'll keep it short."

"She knows she's dead, but she's talking to us anyway." Derry shuddered. "Anyone else creeped out?"

"Quiet." Marita jabbed him. "We're getting to the good stuff."

"Luca isn't a black witch. She's fae. She's also Albert Nádasdy's former lover. He jilted her, she got pissed off, and she's spent decades on her plan to burn Black Hat—and everyone in it—to the ground. If you haven't gotten to the poisonings yet, bully for you. They're coming. And it's going to get ugly. Luca wants paras out in the open. She's going to keep killing humans until they figure out they're not alone in the world."

We had reached that part, and it was ugly. No argument here.

"The director created Black Hat to protect paras from human discovery, right?" She scoffed. *"Wrong."* Her expression darkened. "He created Black Hat to make us believe we were better off flying under the radar. He enforced the narrative we had to hide to be safe. Maybe it's true, or maybe it's not. It doesn't matter what I think. It matters what the para community believes. Luca knows that, and she'll use it."

"Whoa." Colby's eyes rounded. "This is getting good."

"Black Hat isn't a savior or a protector or a guardian. It's a propaganda machine." Her eyes glinted. "Did it ever strike you as strange how, on Nádasdy's crusade to thwart humanity, he only recruited the worst of the worst? People with the least moral fiber? Creatures with the most power? Anyone willing to kill and not sob into their pillow about it later?" She chortled to herself. "He's been recruiting a private army of mercenaries trained to do his bidding, and he's infiltrated every major city in the country. No one batted an eye because he did it out in the open, and he stuck to his mission statement. He did good work, or so he let them believe as he answered their cries for help, using those cases to pad his numbers."

An uneasy silence hummed in the air between us and this digital ghost of Nan.

"Luca is going to throw a wrench in the Bureau's cogs for no other reason than to erase the director's legacy. She believes when the walls come crumbling down, Black Hat will lose its power along with its purpose. All those psychos? Killers? Maneaters? Those you call *agents*? They'll be set free with no one to rein them in." She clicked a few more buttons. "Don't get me wrong, I admire her dedication to erasing an ex from existence, but this has gone too far."

At least we could all agree on that point.

"Listen, I have as many what-ifs as every other para who wonders how different life might be if humans weren't top of the pyramid, but unlike those dreamers, I can read between the lines of human history to predict how very badly this will go for us." She cracked her neck. "The director might be toeing the company line, *his* line, but that doesn't mean he's wrong."

While I appreciated the opinion piece, we needed hard facts. "Are there any files other than this video?"

"Okay." Nan rubbed her face onscreen. "You're tired of me babbling, right?"

"She's good," I admitted. "I *am* tired of her babbling."

"Rude," Marita chided. "This is basically her will."

"Show some respect," Derry chided me. "But yeah, I was starting to get bored there at the end."

"If you want to preserve the status quo," Nan resumed. "You'll need to take out Luca." Her mouth crimped. "Rue Hollis—who you may or may not be—is causing more trouble than Luca anticipated." She sobered. "She's going to double down on my NDA, and goddess only knows what will be left of me then. I'm in too deep to get out." She held a pill up to the camera. "But you can make sure I get mine, even if it's from beyond the grave." She clicked another button. "Files are done loading. Thanks for listening."

"She knew the NDA was coming," I murmured, "but she stuck it out."

"If you're asking why I stuck it out—"

"She's *really* good," Marita interrupted, and I shushed her.

"Luca has my mom. I know, I know. It's not cool for black witches to be sentimental. But Mom buried the family grimoire in an undisclosed location, and I would really like to get my hands on it before she kicks the bucket. For the magic, and for the numbers and passwords to all her offshore accounts."

The message ended with a sly wink from Nan before the screen went dark.

"Here goes nothing." Colby closed that window then opened another. "This is…"

"A bunch of nonsense." I scrunched up my face. "What is this gobbledygook?"

"Code." Asa cut his eyes toward me. "These are programs Nan wrote, including her passwords."

Adrenaline trickled into my veins, pumping me up for the fight to come. "What do they do?"

"I can't tell yet." Colby read line by line, furrowing her brow. "One of these must tell us how to find Luca, but I…" Her concentration grew more intense as she clicked another file. "There's the credit card Nan was using for travel. Boston, Charlotte, Dallas. She was in each city."

"Does that mean Luca let her handle the distribution?" I mulled it over. "If she was doing the legwork for Luca, then who or what has the director been tracking?" I slumped as defeat sank into me, a punishment for getting my hopes up. "Clay was right here. Part of him anyway. I thought for sure…"

Maybe it had been dumb luck and not an indication of some grand plan.

"From here, we can lock Luca out of every single app, program, and database created for her."

Awe surged through me, along with the urge to kiss her puckered brow. "You can do that?"

"Give me a few," Colby mumbled, already deep into her process.

Fergal caught my eye, and I nodded at him to stay. He knew how to be quiet. Colby wouldn't mind him. I didn't care if she did mind, honestly. I might never leave that girl on her own ever again.

ABOUT THE TIME I WAS READY TO CRAWL OUT OF MY SKIN, I GOT A CALL from the cleaners and gritted my teeth.

Had Asa been standing any closer to me, I would have handed my phone off to him.

"Director Hollis speaking." I reined in my growl, tried again. "How can I help you?"

"It would be a great *help* if you didn't lay siege then flee before our arrival."

A snort shot out of Asa's nose that he didn't try to hide as he listened in on the conversation.

"Sorry about that." A wince drew my shoulders toward my ears. "My hands are full these days."

"We're aware." She let me squirm. "We've identified a peculiarity worth mentioning to you."

That must be one heck of a peculiarity for them to call me direct. "Oh?"

"The victim, Nanette Bakersfield, had a lock of strawberry-blonde hair braided into hers."

Nan's hair was black, which meant… "You're sure it wasn't a dye job?"

Folks loved to get streaks in their hair, though they usually went for eye-popping colors.

A sigh blasted the other end of the phone. "There were roots, but they weren't in her scalp."

Roots made tracking spells stick better than cut hair. "Anything else odd about it?"

"A witch on our team says it's saturated with magic that didn't belong to the dead witch."

"How so?"

"It's fae magic."

"Fae magic," I repeated, my mind reeling with possibilities. "I see."

"She's seen it before when a perp wanted to hide their power signature beneath someone else's."

There was bitter irony for you.

We had been tracking Clay's wig, not Clay, and the director had been tracking Luca's braid, not Luca.

"That helps." I wanted to bang my head against the wall. "More than you know."

"The rest of the findings will be uploaded into the database, as usual. I've been in touch with the Kellies, and they're ready to receive from us again. I wouldn't have called, except these things tend to be time sensitive. Since this is evidence in an active case, I was doing my due diligence."

Well, that answered my earlier question.

The call ended before I could express my gratitude.

"Every time we draw a step closer, we get punched in the face and stumble back a mile." I thumped my phone against my forehead. "She has us chasing our tails."

"The director doesn't know that."

"The director—" I pushed the defeat from my mind and paid attention, "—doesn't know he was tracking Nan, not Luca."

Okay.

Think.

The director was tracking Luca. His mention of Charlotte and Dallas was too on point otherwise. Luca had been hiding behind Nan. That was the deal with the braid in Nan's hair. To paint her as the target.

That indicated Luca suspected the director would come after her, and she just might let him.

The ploy might have been intended to buy her time to finalize her plans for him. To set one final trap. To let him rush into it on his own without her lifting a finger to entice him. For all we knew, she had felt the shiver of a bargain fulfilled when Nan set the pill on her tongue.

"Crap." I mashed redial before my hand caught up to my brain. "If we can preserve the braid's magic…"

"Then we can use it to lure the director to us."

A different person answered, which wasn't unusual. Cleaners didn't have personal numbers. They didn't form relationships with the subjects of their cases or the people running the investigations. They strove for a neutrality that was impossible to achieve, but they got closer than any organization I could name.

As soon as a cleaner picked up, I put in a verbal request for custody of the evidence.

A courier would drop it off at our hotel, and I had until then to file the hard copies.

"We don't have long." Asa pivoted toward the door. "We need to gather the others and form a plan."

"We don't know how long ago the director figured out the wig was spelled. It could have been as early as yesterday, after the scuffle at the distillery." I had to say it, had to remind myself not to let my hopes rise too high. "He could be anywhere by now."

"Let's cross our fingers he wants Luca enough to get careless."

We joined the others in the suite shared by the Mayhews and Arden and cobbled together a plan that left me too anxious to sit. I paced the room from end to end, driving everyone insane, but they let me get away with it. Probably because Colby was right with me, gliding from corner to corner, raring to go.

By the time the courier arrived with the braid, Dad had returned, back from checking on Mom.

"This won't help us find Luca." He reached for the plastic sleeve. "She's blocking her true location."

"If we can lure the director to us, we can use him as bait to trap Luca."

Tick, tick, tick.

Every second of wasted time roared in my ears, but we were so close. This had to work. It *had* to.

Since Dad was the one with the magic, I gave him space to begin reading the spell on the braid.

When Fergal indicated we needed to talk, I aimed for the seating area to avoid disturbing Dad.

"I've just heard from Agent Morton in Boston. Isiforos is being restrained in a guest room at The Spinnaker." He kept it short but not so sweet. "He was torturing the Kellies with his Miserae powers when he was apprehended."

"That makes no sense." I sank down onto the bed. "Why would he do that?"

"Morton says Isiforos was coordinating the cleanup efforts at ground zero via video chat with the team leader when he got a call. He stood, left the chat going, and pressed his hand to the door leading into the ballroom where the Kellies have been sequestered. A minute later, their screams alerted the other agents on duty, who captured him."

"Has anyone questioned him?"

"He claims to have no memory of the incident."

"Make sure they don't hurt him." I put steel behind the order. "I can't believe he would do this on his own."

"You think he's been spelled?"

"We had a wig with a chauffeur cruising around Dallas, and this is what stretches your imagination?"

"Fair point." He cleared his throat. "What would you like me to do?"

That was the tricky part. I wasn't sure. But I didn't have the luxury of meditating on it.

"Take Arden and return to Boston." I turned it over in my head. "Find a black witch who specializes in mental manipulation. There should be plenty on the payroll." Abuse of that knowledge was usually what landed those witches in the Bureau. "Get them to sweep Isiforos, see if they detect any abnormalities."

"All right." Fergal hesitated. "Are you sure you want me to bring Arden?"

For him to ask, she must not be on speaking terms with him again.

"We're about to set a trap for the director. I would consider it a personal favor if she wasn't here."

Besides, the forced proximity would leave Arden no choice but to engage him. A much healthier solution than him leaving her behind to stew over the sharp reminder of his nature.

"Will you fetch Miss Colby, or would you prefer I escort her?"

"Miss Colby, huh?" I smothered a snort. "That kid works fast."

Already, she had Fergal wrapped around her little finger.

"She's a remarkable child," he huffed, clearly affronted. "What would you have me call her?"

"She responds well to *Captain*," I teased, enjoying someone else being in the dark for once.

"I'll gather the *captain*'s things and see you shortly," he said dryly.

As I tapped the cell against my chin, I couldn't stop myself from making a leap that explained a *lot*.

Angling my head toward Asa, I had to ask, "Are you thinking what I'm thinking?"

"That Isiforos was the one who put the phone in the director's hand?"

"Yes."

"Assuming he was compromised, and his actions weren't his own, who got to him?"

"I'm not sure." I folded my arms across my middle. "I'm more concerned about *when*."

The knowledge I had reached out, finally trusted someone, and ended up here sat heavy in my gut.

Isiforos wasn't to blame, but that didn't change the fact he was a threat to us until we figured this out.

"Do you think Luca orchestrated it?" Asa vibrated with tension. "The director's escape?"

"We can't afford to rule it out."

"We need to find out who called Isiforos. Colby can handle it while the Kellies recover."

The phone connection bugged me, seeing as how that was how Clay got snared. But he was a golem. He was bound to his master's wishes. Which, now that I thought about it, could explain Isiforos's behavior if it was a verbal command that activated him.

"I wonder if Nan told her. About the Kellies. Nan was her right-hand woman, so she would have noticed when the Bureau's database went from flatlining to active." I let my head fall back. "If Luca was behind Isiforos putting the phone in the director's hand, I could see why she sent him after the Kellies. She had to be worried how much they knew and chose to take them out before they could be used against her."

"Without Nan, Luca won't be able to track the Kellies moving forward."

"Chances are Luca won't know if the hit on the Kellies succeeded either. If the commands on Isiforos are voice activated—" I shared my new theory with him, "—she could have called to tell him what to do, but she would have no guarantee he followed orders."

"The way she used Nan as an errand girl, Nan might have been the one in control."

There was also the fact Luca was fae. As much as she enjoyed playing dress-up with black witches, she wasn't one. If the spell on Isiforos had dark magic roots, Luca couldn't have cast it herself.

So who had?

CHAPTER SIXTEEN

Colby rode into our room on Arden's head, bundled in her blanket, while Arden carried the laptop.

Out in the hall, phone pressed to his ear, Fergal made travel arrangements for their return to Boston.

"Nan bought tickets for two more flights," Colby announced. "Denver and L.A."

"That gives us a time frame." I nodded along. "A chance to get the word out to both cities."

Dallas happened too quickly for us to spare them, but we could get ahead of Luca this time.

"We can check the database," Asa suggested. "See what covens are operating in or near those cities."

"No need." Colby grinned at him. "Nan kept a copy of her contacts' information."

"That's amazing. We can send agents to intercept the rogues and shut down distribution in the new cities before it begins. Make sure Boston, Charlotte, and Dallas also get copies." I dared to be optimistic. "Any luck on narrowing down Luca's location?"

"Not yet." Her antennae drooped. "Nan was in contact with her, so I'll figure it out."

So far, the Kellies hadn't turned up any useful leads on real estate, but it was hard to blame them when half their job was rebuilding all that had been lost. For every step they took forward, their new equipment and resources set them back two.

"Never doubted it." I pressed my lips to the top of her head. "You're the smartest moth girl I know."

To evade us this long, the director must be paying in cash and staying off grid to avoid detection. That, I was sad to say, was likely Clay's doing. He was a much more dangerous choice in bodyguard if for no other reason than he was in tune with the modern world and how technology worked. Unlike Bjorn.

"I'm the only moth girl you know." She rolled her eyes. "Can you set me up on the couch?"

The way she clung to her blanket, unwilling to let it drop even for a short flight, gutted me all over again.

Once she was settled in, I brought Arden in for a hug. "Be safe and listen to Fergal."

"I will." She squeezed me tight. "Are you sure you don't want me to stay?"

The edge of nerves in her voice wasn't as sharp as I had feared it would be, and that made it easier to stick to my guns. She had to sort this out with Fergal. To stay in this world, even to keep a toe in, she must learn to accept creatures for who they are and not romanticize them.

"I appreciate the offer, but I would feel better if you weren't here for what comes next."

"I understand." She laughed at my expression. "What?" She released me. "I can be reasonable."

Hoping that remained true, I told Fergal, "Keep me updated on the Isiforos situation."

"I'll let you know as soon as the witch is finished with him."

The two of them left, and I rolled my shoulders, relieving the tension.

As my muscles loosened the tiniest bit, I spied Dad prowling toward us and seized up again.

Oh well.

Maybe when this was over, I could sweet-talk Asa into giving me a massage.

A full-body massage.

Mmm.

Or maybe I could just crawl in bed, snuggle into him, and sleep for a month. A year. A decade?

So many of my fantasies lately involved the two of us together, in bed and…unconscious.

Not the steamiest daydream for a newly engaged couple for sure.

"I've done what I can to sustain its magic." Dad strode in with the braid in his fist. "A spell of this type feeds off its host's energy. It had absorbed enough of Nan's essence for me to revive it, but within the next six to ten hours, it will begin giving off my signature instead of Luca's."

Oh fun. Another ticking clock. Now the others would have a new friend to play with.

"How do we guarantee the director comes to us before then?"

"Asa makes a good point." I leaned my shoulder against him. "We blew the wig test."

There was no telling what precautions the director had taken, but the wig wouldn't have been sent on a joyride without having a means of tracking its movements. He would know, or suspect, the driver was dead after he saw the car had been stationary for several hours.

"All we can do is stay put and hope that piques the director's interest enough he gets bold." Dad dipped his chin. "Now that Father has disposed of the spell on Clay, ensuring we can't track his movements, our blind spot might prove enough of a temptation for him to pursue Luca, even if doubling back in this area is a risky proposition."

But while we were playing Luca to lure him in, where was the real one?

"We're wasting time." I raked my fingers through my hair, yanking on the roots like that might tear out clumps of guilt instead of my scalp. "Innocent lives pay for every second we burn."

Both humans and the denizens of Hael.

"This isn't a waste of time." Dad cupped my elbow, leading me to the door. "Neither is this."

Asa shifted his weight forward, ready to follow, but Dad pressed a hand against his chest.

"I want to work on her magic." Dad slid his gaze past Asa's shoulder. "It's best if we do that alone."

The intensity of Asa's stare as it settled on me almost buckled my knees, but he let it go. "All right."

"Want to make out before I leave?" I fisted his shirt in my free hand. "Make Dad regret his life choices?"

A smile teased the edge of his lips, as I hoped it would, but he shook his head. "I'll stay with Colby."

Since I would much rather her stay here, and safe, while Dad threw magic at me, I smiled. "Thanks."

"Come on." Dad held the door. "We don't have long, but I promised your mother I would make time."

With Colby back with me, I had let the priority of the Hunk slide down the to-do list yet again. I was grateful Dad was throwing on the brakes, forcing me to take a moment for myself, even as life spun out around me. It was nice being taken care of, and not just by my friends and chosen family, but by my actual parents.

They had missed so many milestones in my life through no fault of their own, and I was grateful that this was when they had been returned to me. I was happy they could glimpse who I wanted to be, not who I had been raised to be. Happy they could meet Colby and Asa. Happy we could heal the wounds of our pasts together, even if it meant opening old scars first.

We entered the elevator and rode it to the top floor. The fancy lock on the door leading to the roof was no match for Dad's magic, and I let myself out. A moment of hesitation as Dad joined me warned he had more on his mind than magic and wanted privacy to discuss it. "Colby shouldn't be there if we have to fight Clay."

The idea of wounding Clay opened a hole in my chest that sucked all the air from my lungs.

No wonder Dad wanted to have this talk out of her earshot. Truthfully? I didn't want to hear it either.

"All we have to do is smudge his *shem*." I gripped Dad's arm. "We need to neutralize him, not hurt him."

The hard edges of Dad's expression softened as his gaze settled on me. "I'll do my best to only immobilize him."

I narrowed my eyes on him to drive home the point I expected his best to be more than good enough.

"I'll text Marita and Derry." I pursed my lips. "We'll need the backup if Clay shows."

As much as I hated agreeing with Dad, I knew he was right to be cautious.

And that just plain sucked.

TRUE TO HIS WORD, DAD HAD DECIDED TO WORK ON MY MAGIC. JUST not on the roof. He and Colby had used the tablet to virtually scout a field outside of town. Might as well be productive while we waited to see if the director took the bait. The field put distance between us and potential casualties if things took a turn for the worse with our trap, or my magic.

Dad had also decided the rural location wouldn't scream *trap* the way the warehouse district or a nice, abandoned building strung with floor-to-ceiling cobwebs and spiced with broken windows might.

"I'm going to cast a ward to conceal us from passersby." Dad walked a perfect circle with a circumference of twenty feet or so using salt as a marker. "That should give us plenty of room."

Based on all the times Clay had attempted to part me from the Hunk, I kept my expectations low.

As Dad's magic domed over our heads, and the outside world took on the wavy quality of antique glass, the familiar prickle of magic stung my palms like limbs slowly waking after they had fallen asleep.

"I've been studying the flow of your ambient magic since Lake

Pontchartrain. Your mother has been cross-referencing my notes and doing her own research while she's been with Meg."

"So that's why the contract is taking so long. I figured they were just hanging out."

Given how long it had been since they spent time with one another, I wouldn't have blamed them.

"Until you're free of this blight, your mother won't be 'hanging out,' and neither will Meg. The prognosis from Proctor, and Asa's grandmother, has led us to believe we have six months or less. The Hunk will kill you if we don't break its hold over you, and it won't stop trying until it succeeds."

"Six months?" I rubbed my hands up my arms. "That's...not great."

This was what ignoring my problems got me. They hadn't gone away. I had just given them more time to plot against me.

"Between the three of us, we have a theory of where the artifact planted roots in you." He meshed his fingers. "The issue is the depth they've grown around the core of your power. There are multiple anchor points, solidifying its hold over you."

"You can still read my magic, even with me bound?"

"That's what gave me the idea for this, actually, but I've been studying you for some time."

"Okay?"

"Your magic is strong, and it fills you to the brink. Think of it as a river. Vast. Deep. But the binding dams up that energy until the water runs dry. Except the Hunk is chipping away at the dam, and so does Colby. There are cracks spreading, and moisture is leaking, faster and faster. The places with the worst damage are the seven chakra points, where the Hunk is trying its hardest to form permanent tethers."

"And it's easier to track one piddly stream at a time than it is a river full of tributaries."

"Exactly."

"I assume since you warned me about the multiple anchor points, this is going to hurt."

"Yes." His amusement waned. "It will feel as if someone is trying to rip the magic from your body."

"Because that's what's happening." I winced. "Gotcha."

"We don't have to do this." He rested a hand on my shoulder. "We can try other methods first."

"Other methods haven't worked so far." I shook out my hands. "I'm ready. Really. I can handle it."

The now-familiar expression of intense study he wore while following the threads of complex spells settled over his features. I could tell when he quit seeing me and the magic revealed itself to him.

Much as we had done at the cabin where the director had fled, he reached out and hooked his fingers in the air. His hand was six inches from my heart. Somehow, I wasn't surprised to learn that was the seat of the infection.

"I'm sorry," he exhaled, a glimmer in his eyes.

And then he yanked.

A lurch in my chest, a thud in my ears, and my eyes rolled back in my head.

CHAPTER SEVENTEEN

Softly fading notes of an old lullaby tickled the edges of my memories. No. Not a memory.

The rich voice singing rasped to a final hoarse note that was too raw to be fogged by time.

"Your mother will kill me if you don't open your eyes soon."

Pain radiated through every part of me. Every. Single. Inch. Even the ends of my hair hurt.

Slowly, I propped open my eyes and got a face full of Dad, who was cradling me in the dirt. "Ouch."

"How do you feel?" His grip tightened around me. "Are you still in pain?"

"Crunchy." I smacked my lips. "And yes."

Apparently, when your own magic got cut off and someone else filled you with theirs like a vase, the end result was your insides burnt to a crisp. I could now sympathize with pellet grills everywhere.

Splaying his fingers, Dad gripped the ball of my shoulder and pushed healing magic into me.

The faint taste of hydrangeas hit the back of my throat as he channeled Mom's magic, and stupid tears prickled the backs of my eyes as sweet relief coasted over me.

"I warned your mother I wasn't a healer." He jerked his hand back. "Should we—?"

"It's not that." I sniffled. "I can feel Mom. In your magic." I wiped my face with the back of my hand. "It's just...nice. Knowing she's still with us. That you guys get some kind of happily ever after."

Not the one they deserved, but I doubted either of them would complain about the nature of their second chance.

"None of us have had time to fully appreciate what you've done for your mother, and me."

"One foot in front of the other." I let him help me into a seated position. "We can feel our feels later."

If that last part confused Dad, well, that made two of us.

The world spun and dipped as I righted myself and coughed up a smoky aftertaste.

A prickle in my palm convinced me I had planted it in an ant bed, and I jerked my hand against my chest.

"What's wrong?" Dad gripped my wrist, his expression tight. "Your magic is waking."

"Can you tell if you loosened the Hunk?"

"There are seven anchors," he reminded me, "one in each of your chakras."

"How many did you remove?"

The seam of his lips gathered into a purse. "One."

"Oh." I tested myself, marveling at how well Dad had channeled Mom's pure energy into healing me. "Do you think we have time to go again?" I checked my phone. "I was out for what? Thirty minutes?"

A glimmer of pride spread across his features before a darker emotion tempered it.

"I wish it didn't have to be this way." He cradled my cheek. "I vowed the day Howl told me she was expecting that I would never harm our child. I haven't honored that promise."

"You and I understand better than she ever will, what it was like being raised by the director." I covered his hand with mine. "You're not like him." A phantom twinge in my hand where he used to rap my knuckles with his cane made them ache. "You're not cruel for the sake of being cruel. You're not hurting me out of spite. You're helping me. And if it hurts, well, then, it hurts."

The pain was worth ridding myself of the parasitic Hunk for good.

"One more," he agreed when it became clear I wasn't letting the matter drop. "That's it."

"For today."

"Your mother is going to have words for me," he muttered, his gaze swinging skyward.

"I'll handle Mom." I considered how we began and where I ended up waking. "Should I lie down?"

Before he nodded, I had made up my mind. I didn't need to make this any more stressful for either of us.

"Are you ready?" His exhale whistled through his teeth. "I'll choose a lesser one this time."

With a jerk of my chin, I prepared myself for the pain to swallow me whole.

Lucky for me, I blacked out before I felt the first tug.

A TICKLE BRUSHED ACROSS MY UPPER LIP AS CONSCIOUSNESS PAID ME A reluctant visit.

"Quit that."

"Haven't you heard of smelling salts?"

More grains sprinkled over me.

"Smelling salts. Not *smell* salt. Table salt doesn't work."

"Derry?" I choked when my mouth flooded with granules. "Marita?"

"Ha." Marita patted my cheek. "I told you it would work, Derriere."

"Here." Derry pressed something cold into my hand. "Rinse out your mouth."

As my eyes got on board with the idea of opening, I got an eyeful of naked warg on either side of me.

I decided it was best to shut my eyes until the view improved, but I let Marita angle my head for a sip.

"You've seen my boobs before." Marita forced open one of my eyes. "Stop being a baby."

"It's not that." I gurgled as she poured liquid down my throat. *"Marita."*

"You're the problem," she blamed Derry. "Your junk is too close to her elbow."

Jerking my arm in tighter against my chest, I shoved upright, spluttering and hacking. "Where's Dad?"

"A black car has driven around the block twice." Derry backed up to give me room. "He's investigating."

"We heard the screams," Marita explained before I could ask, "and we came running."

"Thanks," I rasped, my throat thick with emotion—and mucus. "You guys are the best."

"Remember that after we get your faux bestie back."

Her certainty choked me up for another reason entirely.

"We *will* get him back." Derry misread my quiet for distress. "I promise you that."

A fresh wave of dizziness swept through me, prompting me to ask, "Did Dad leave any instructions?"

"Only if you died on our watch, he would rip our tails out through our jaws." Derry snorted. "Funny guy."

"He wasn't joking," Marita and I said at the same time.

As I sat there, I ran an inventory of aches and pains, determining if I could sense…well…anything.

"What was he doing?" Marita braced me when I swayed. "Unlocking your magic?"

"He can't do that." Derry yawned. "The Hunk would take her over, remember?"

"I meant unlocking the Hunk from her magic, obviously."

"Yeah." I couldn't decide what the tingles in my limbs meant, and without magic to call on, I couldn't check the threads for answers either. "He figured out how to remove it." I rubbed my chest. "Or loosen it anyway." I winced at a faint twinge. "Time will tell."

"You sounded like someone was ripping your soul out of your

body." Marita helped me onto my feet. "Are you sure you want to keep going?"

"The alternative is going my whole life without magic." I grimaced as she helped me walk toward where Dad must have gone. "Even if he does nothing but lessen its hold, I'll get a reprieve."

On the other hand, with magic already eroding the bindings, if we didn't act, the Hunk might kill me first.

"Are you sure it would be safe to use magic then?" Derry kept pace with us. "It sounds dangerous."

"Dad won't lift the binding unless he thinks I can handle it." A smile crept up on me. "Mom would throttle him otherwise."

A slow burn spread down my arms and into my hands, but I wasn't calling magic.

"You okay?" Marita quit walking to check me. "You look pale."

"I've got that same feeling like when I knew we had to go to Charlotte."

"I can guess why." Head tipped back, Derry scented the air. "We've got company."

"Please don't tell me Asa caved and brought Colby out here."

"You ask people not to tell you things—a *lot*—but you don't leave us much wiggle room, and I'm too hungry to get creative." He rubbed his stomach. "Yes, it's Asa. And yes, Colby is with him."

Five minutes later, Asa prowled into our midst, and Colby glided to the top of the nearest tree.

"If you were anyone else," he said, warm eyes locked on mine after checking Colby was out of hearing range. "I would question finding you laid out in a clearing with a naked married couple."

Oops.

Guess he saw that part.

And here I had been hoping he only spotted us after I got my legs working again.

"We would have waited until you arrived if we had known you were coming." Marita batted her lashes. "You guys ready for round two?"

Derry turned his back on us, hunched his shoulders, and cupped his junk.

"Not sure if he's turned on at the idea of swinging with you guys, or if he's that afraid Asa might break off his pee-pee if he so much as pretends to go along with the gag." She let Asa take over supporting me. "To be on the safe side, we'll begin our changes. He always feels safer freeballing it when he's got fangs."

Happy to lean into Asa, I raised an eyebrow at Marita. "I'm starting to think you just like saying pee-pee."

"We have a nephew who's potty training," Derry explained. "Marita has become a little *too* invested in his success."

"There's a betting pool," she countered. "Picking up potty training lingo is a small sacrifice when the prize is all you can eat ribs from Merle's Meat Shack."

"I found Saint." Colby landed on top of my head. "He's to the right, about half a mile out."

"Marita mentioned a black car?" I smiled when she leaned over my forehead to see me. "Before you ask me, I'm fine. I have some good news even. Dad has figured out how to free me from the Hunk. Probably. We're taking it slow, but it's the most progress anyone has made since this started."

No one had been willing to hurt me enough to try, though plenty of folks had suggested death as a solution. It wasn't fair this unsavory task fell to Dad, but he was the equivalent of a surgeon when it came to his precision with black magic. If anyone had a shot at removing this tumorous growth, it was him.

"That is good news." She sniffed then coughed. "You smell like burnt hair."

"Yeah." I wrinkled my nose. "The binding is causing magic to go haywire when it hits my system."

Gentling his hold on me, Asa tucked me in closer. "Do you want to wait for your father?"

"Do you mind scouting one more time, Colby?" I wanted to buy a moment with Asa. "Look for the car."

Colby shot into the air, determination shining in her dark eyes.

"You're hurt worse than you want Colby to know." Asa read me with ease. "How can I help?"

"Dad can channel Mom. He patched me up after he removed the first anchor. He can do it again."

When his confusion became evident, I explained Dad's revelation about chakra points to him.

"What happens when the last anchor is gone?"

"Hopefully, the Hunk shrivels and falls off my neck like a cauterized skin tag."

"As evocative as that description is, I would prefer a more concrete answer before we reach that point."

"There are several more to go." I checked on Colby. "Dad has a baseline reading of my normal magic and my bound magic. He'll examine me between rounds to make sure all is going according to plan."

The pinch of his lips betrayed how much he wanted to argue against it, but he knew as well as I did we had no better options.

A thunderous *boom* shook the ground under us, and a pillar of flames gouted into the sky.

Something told me Colby would have no trouble locating the car now.

"I see the car." Colby swooped overhead before settling on my shoulder. "The engine is smoking."

Yep.

Sometimes I hate being right.

Beside me, Asa gave way to Blay, who cracked his knuckles.

Antennae aquiver, Colby readied for takeoff. "I'll go—"

"No." I cupped my hand over her wings. "Stay close until we figure out who's behind the wheel."

"Okay." A shiver rippled through her she couldn't quite contain before she locked down her fear. "Can I try something?" She read my unease and hardened her expression. "I can heal you. Not through the familiar bond. Just me. *Loinnir* magic." Her fluff stood on end. "Will you let me?"

Clay had warned me that once our familiar bond was cemented, there was no going back. Colby had to use her magic, or it would build up and kill her. I wasn't sure how that worked now that our connection was clogged, but I figured better safe than sorry.

"I would appreciate that." I eased away from Blay. "Just don't hurt yourself in the process."

A subtle warmth pulsed under my skin where she sat, spreading through my body like a sigh.

The aches and pains dulled to manageable levels, and I blew out a long breath of relief.

"That's incredible." I smooched the side of her head. "I feel like a new woman."

"See?" She was winded but smiling. "I did it." Her wings drooped, and she melted onto my shoulder. "I'm fine." She threw off my attempts to help, her breaths coming fast. "I just need to rest for a second."

Either the kink in our bond or the sheer amount of damage I had done to myself, via the Hunk, had put a bigger strain on her than usual. "Rest all you want."

"Blay protect Colby." He reached for her, and she reclined across his open palms. "Blay keep her safe."

"Thanks, big guy." I ran my fingers through his hair. "I'm going to check on Dad."

"Blay come too." He walked with Colby caged between his thick fingers. "Rue not go alone."

A short yip brought my attention swinging back to the pair of wolves with tongues lolling.

"I won't be alone," I promised him. "The Mayhews will protect me."

With that, Marita bared her teeth in a vicious grin, clearly on board with the plan.

Beside her, Derry snapped his jaws, allowing drool to slide down his chin.

Which he flung at Marita before bounding away at breakneck speed.

Strings of slobber crisscrossing her face, Marita bristled from head to toe and gave chase.

Oy.

This was not shaping up to be the stealth mission I envisioned, but that was wargs for you.

"Rue sure Derry wolf and Marita wolf keep Rue safe?"

"We'll be fine." I peeked in at a sleeping Colby one last time. "Stay put, and we'll be right back."

"Rue scream if Rue needs Blay." He sat with his back against a tree. "Blay come to rescue."

Warmed inside and out, I smiled at him. "Thank—"

"Just like Boom Hammer in Super Mystics."

"Colby has been back five minutes, and you're already spouting infomercials."

"Boom Hammer swings a gods-blessed hammer that can smash through *anything*."

"I notice you two never mention the price."

"You can't put a price on happiness."

The sincerity with which he delivered the line had me peering closer at the moth in his hands, but she was out cold.

"We'll discuss this later," I promised Blay. "Then you can tell me all about this newest expansion pack."

Ever since Mystic Realms released its first spin-off, they kept coming faster and faster.

How did they expect kids to keep up with the expense of purchasing the latest editions?

Oh.

Right.

They knew exactly who would foot the bill.

Parents.

And who would be at the head of the line? Me. I tended to do better with showing my emotion through purchases made under duress, so this latest expansion pack had timed its release well.

Over the tears my credit card wept in fear of the coming charges, I imagined I heard mothy cackles.

CHAPTER EIGHTEEN

The Mayhews and I padded toward the fiery remains of a black car identical to the one used to drive the wig around Dallas. Eager to search for clues before they were consumed by flames, I got three feet away before another blast rocked the metal frame.

"Stand back." I retreated to a safe distance before the fire could melt off my face. "Goddess."

There would be no evidence left in that smoldering mass, no hints as to where its occupants had gone.

A glint in the distance caught my eye, and I rocked forward, seconds from launching a pursuit.

Marita and Derry stepped in front of me, their furry bodies penning me in, refusing to budge an inch.

"For all we know, that could be the director." I shoved them, but they didn't cave to my pleas. "He's getting away."

The wargs shook their heads, growling softly at me, then Derry broke away.

"I don't have access to my magic, but I'm not useless." I set my jaw at Marita. "I can still fight."

She set a paw on my foot, I thought to comfort me, but she was staring past me.

Following her line of sight, I swallowed as a rock dropped into my stomach.

Clay.

He was here. Right there. Behind me.

Our gazes clashed and then held for an eternity I spent searching for any hint of my friend. Neat rows furrowed his brow as he stared at me. Maybe he was doing the same. Looking for answers within me.

Stubborn hope I had never quite managed to stamp out resurfaced. He didn't know me. I knew that. I *knew* it. I wasn't delusional enough to believe I could talk to him, break through to him, but I stood there with my heart in my eyes for as long as he could stand it before ripping his attention away to assess the other threats.

"That's Rue." Derry walked up behind me on two legs. "She's your best friend."

Clay didn't speak, but he didn't attack or flee either. That was a good sign, right?

"She was your partner once, at Black Hat." Derry held his ground. "Do you remember?"

"This is ridiculous." I kept crushing my hope, grinding it down to dust. "You're wasting your breath."

"*Rue.*"

The buzz in my ears kept me from pinpointing who, exactly, was yelling my name.

"Colby not in Blay's hand." Blay ran a zigzag pattern, tracing her evasive maneuvers. "Colby get Blay in *big* trouble."

I should have warned him not to trust her where Clay was concerned. The kid was as loyal as they came. I shouldn't have believed she would hang back when there was the slightest chance of recovering him.

"Clay," Colby hollered at him. "Do you remember me?"

The tension drained out of him, and he stood there, transfixed by her. "Moth girl."

A pinch of hurt pleated her features when he didn't call her by name, but she soldiered on.

"That's right." She pirouetted above his head, careful to remain out of reach. "Did you miss me?"

"I…" Clay cocked his head to one side. "Moth girl left." His lips pulled down into a frown. "I was. Glad."

The broken language confused me when Clay had always sounded like a detached version of himself in the past. Not that he had spoken to me, exactly, but I had heard him converse with the director often.

Catching Blay's eye, I motioned for him to hold steady while she tried reasoning with Clay.

"I was glad too, but when I got home, I missed Clay. I missed *you*. I had to come see you."

"Clay," he repeated. "I'm not. Clay. He's. Not me."

Muscle flickered in his jaw, and he clenched his hands, but he couldn't get out the rest. That was when I understood. He was fighting. For her. Clay, the *real* Clay, was doing his best to claw his way out.

How? How was this possible? How could he defy orders?

"You *are* Clay." Colby fluffed into a sphere of white fuzz. "The director doesn't want you to remember, but you do. I can tell. Otherwise, you wouldn't have hidden me from him. You knew I was in danger from him, and you protected me. That wasn't following orders. That was following your heart."

"Moth girl…" He wet his lips. "Go be. Safe. With. Your friends."

"*You* are my friend," she insisted, refusing to back down. "Part of you knows that."

"Col…by." He gripped both sides of his head. "I don't…" He hit his knees. "I can't…"

"Clay?" I stumbled forward, numbed by shock. "Is that really you?"

"Stop me," he panted. "Please." He dug his fingers into his scalp. "Don't let him…"

"I understand," I rasped, my heart beating in the roof of my mouth.

"Bjorn." He choked on the name. "He…"

Pungent magic filled my lungs as Dad joined us, and his presence snapped the tether on the golem.

An agonized roar burst out of Clay, and his arms fell to his sides as he rose wearing a smooth expression. There was no recognition in him now. Just a blank mask and a jut of determination in his chin.

Oh, yeah.

This wasn't good.

The director must have ordered him to take down Dad if he got a chance, and here was an opportunity.

"We need to smudge his *shem*." I marked the symbol with a finger on my forehead for the wargs' sakes. "Break those lines, and he'll freeze like a troll exposed to sunlight."

Magic would have made this easier, but oh well. I wasn't afraid to get my hands dirty. I could do this, with or without that extra zing in my touch. I had to believe that, to trust that I was enough on my own.

The Mayhews waited until the golem burst into motion to charge him. Marita knocked her shoulder into his as Derry mule kicked the bend of his knees. The golem fell sideways but ducked into a roll that kept a grinning Marita from connecting her fist with his face.

Before he straightened to his full height, I leapt onto his back. Impact was like jumping off a bridge into a dry creek bed, but I held on, linking my arms around his throat and my legs around his sides.

"Rue." Dad launched skyward, but he was too late to stop me. "Let him go."

"Not until I finish this." I got my hand as high as the golem's cheek before he clamped down on my wrists. "Do your worst." I stretched my fingers, reaching higher. "I can hang here all day."

A cough exploded out of me when my back hit the dirt. Wait. Dirt? He had flung me over his shoulder so fast, I hadn't seen it coming. I felt it, though.

Ouch.

I jerked my head higher in time to see Dad arrow into Clay's spine, knocking him onto his hands and knees. Dad clung to his back, reached around, and raked elongated claws across Clay's forehead.

The change was instant and heartbreaking as Clay froze on the spot, stuck until we redrew his *shem*.

Colby lit on his bald head, spread her wings wide, and hugged as much of him as she could hold.

"When it's time," she hiccupped, tears in her voice, "I want to reanimate him. I remember how."

Eyes downcast, Blay positioned himself behind Clay, watching over Colby in her grief.

"You've done it before?" Dad climbed off Clay. "Drawn his *shem?*"

"I taught her to the last time he was damaged." I had been so proud of her. "What are you thinking?"

"That a *loinnir* is a remarkable being," he mused. "Colby's love for Clay must have been etched into each stroke. She left a mark on him. On his soul. Not enough to override my father's command, but perhaps it tethered some fragment of Clay's consciousness to his body."

"If anyone could do it, it's Colby." I never ceased being amazed by her. "She loves him as much as she loves me."

"The reverse is also true." Dad surprised me by giving Clay that much credit. "Her power, if that's what caused this, couldn't have stuck if he didn't feel the same."

"How do we move him?" I crouched next to Clay and rested my hand on his shoulder, tempted to follow Colby's lead and throw my arms around him. "He needs to be kept somewhere safe until we can wake him."

"I have an idea." Marita had shifted back while I rode Clay like a bucking bronco. "You might not like it."

Short on time and options, I spread my hands. "I'm open to suggestions."

"We can schedule a pickup for storage." She drew a hand through her hair. "Have him bubble wrapped for his safety and everything. He can be taken to a secure facility until you're ready."

The secure facility was where I had sent my collection of dark artifacts for safe keeping. I didn't want them on me, and most couldn't be destroyed. Like the Hunk. The best I could do was keep them out of circulation.

Never in a million years had I envisioned Clay joining those odds and ends in my personal vault.

"*No.*" Colby sent her antennae bouncing with the force of her head shaking. "You can't do that."

"He won't know." I rested a hand on her back. "He's not aware of what's happening now, and I promise we won't fix his *shem* until we can take him somewhere nice to wake up. Maybe even back home. Or on the farm."

"You're sure he won't wake up?" She didn't loosen her grip a fraction. "I don't want him to think he's alone or that we forgot him. He might get scared if he doesn't know we're coming back."

The scars of her past, the reminder of what the Silver Stag had done to her, ached when she was upset. I could see the similarities between then and now and why she wanted assurances Clay wouldn't suffer as she had.

"He won't even blink until you fix him." I gently scooped her into my palm. "I don't want to leave him behind either, but I would feel better if I knew he was safe."

"You're *sure* he'll be okay?" She searched my face. "You *promise* he'll sleep through this?"

"I give you my word, little one." Dad stepped forward. "Golems are empty shells without magic to act as a conduit for their energy."

"He's *not* a shell, and he's *not* empty." Tears rolled down her furry cheeks. "He's just sleeping."

"I apologize." Dad pressed a hand over his heart. "I misspoke."

While Marita made the necessary arrangements, which entailed her and Derry hanging back until after a hauler arrived for Clay, Dad and I walked under a tree to discuss next moves. Colby, who hadn't forgiven me for agreeing to send Clay away, sat with him while we waited.

Had she seen this before, she would understand this was his time of peace. It was after he woke, after he learned what he had done, that guilt and remorse seeped in until he drowned in his own helplessness.

"I saw someone." I broke the silence. "He was spry for the director."

"I don't see the director allowing himself to be deposited into a field, so it must have been a driver who got spooked when I detonated the car."

"That would explain the running away."

"You didn't pursue him?"

"Too risky."

"You understand," he said slowly, feeling out the words, "that what I said earlier…about you being defenseless against my father…" His gaze swung to mine. "Your magic doesn't define you."

"Thanks, Dad, but no. It wasn't that. Clay turned up before I got very far, and I couldn't risk turning my back on him." I stood straighter. "That reminds me. How do I look magic-wise?"

"The second anchor came free, but it cost you." He shook his head. "I'm not sure we should proceed."

A distant ringing noise clamped my jaw shut while I listened for its origin.

Before I could pinpoint it, Blay jogged over with Asa's phone in his hand and passed it to me.

"Where is your phone?" Arden scowled at me through the screen on video chat. "We called and called."

"I didn't hear it ring." I patted myself down but didn't feel it either. "I must have dropped it."

"I have it." Dad presented it to me. "It fell out of your pocket." He grimaced. "It was smoking."

"That would explain why I missed the call." I couldn't power it on. "Your magic fried it?"

"Mine, the Hunk's, or some combination of the two."

"Lovely." I shoved it into my back pocket, returning my attention to Arden. "What's up?"

"Now that I know you're alive?" Her brow wrinkled. "Fergal is ready for you."

"Isiforos." I pinched the bridge of my nose. "The Kellies."

I hadn't forgotten them but having my brain lightly broiled had toasted my immediate thoughts.

We had time before the transport arrived to fetch Clay, so I found a nice tree and sat with my back against the trunk while she passed the phone over to Fergal, whose pinched expression didn't bode well.

Concern bubbling up for Isiforos, I broke the ice. "What did the witch have to say?"

"He confirmed Isiforos was acting under a geas. Isiforos has no memory of his actions. He was shocked when we played the security footage for him and he saw himself perpetrate the crimes."

"How was he spelled?"

"The tattoo he got in Beverly was a Trojan horse. Based on that particular spell, a short phrase was likely used to activate him. Once he heard it, he would have been receptive to orders. He would have snapped out of it after completing the task he was given."

Thumping my head against the tree, I called myself ten kinds of fool for it never crossing my mind the tattoo was malicious. Well, in more ways than one. It had led us right into a trap, caging us in Faerie while the compound was brought to its knees, and I had assumed that had fulfilled its purpose.

"Does this mean he was the one who put the director on the phone with Clay?"

An activation phrase meant he could have been deployed multiple times before his actions drew notice. Much like Clay, he would have lost his free will when his master took the reins. He would have followed orders to the letter. Including not remembering what he had done, if that was what they wanted from him.

"He can't recall the specifics," he gently reminded me, "but it seems likely."

"As likely as him being the reason we're missing a guard? Luca must have had Isiforos create a scapegoat to maintain his place in our inner circle for as long as possible."

Having witnessed the aftereffects of Clay coming to, learning what he had done under the director's influence, and then having to make his peace with it, I felt sick on Isiforos's behalf.

"How do we neutralize it?"

"The witch says the tattoo must be removed, magically, to destroy the compulsion."

As sacred as tattoos were to Miserae daemons, I regretted the necessity, but we had to stem this tide.

"Do it." I would bear the weight of the decision and the burden of his anger once he was himself again. "He's too great of a security risk otherwise."

"There's one more thing."

"There always is." I wondered if I was too young to retire yet. "What else?"

"Bjorn was released from his cell."

Understanding crashed into me, reminding me of what Clay had tried to tell us.

A bitter pill stuck in my throat, making it hard to swallow. "Isiforos?"

"I spoke to Agent Merkle, the guard on duty. He received a direct order via email from Isiforos shortly before the attack on the Kellies. Isiforos must have sent it during the chat before the attack."

A troubling thought stirred in me, and I leaned forward. "How long ago was this?"

"Six hours, give or take." He hesitated. "We weren't notified because Bjorn's off the books."

We hadn't wanted a paper trail that the director's loyalists could follow to free his number-one stooge. As usual, what at first seemed like a good idea had bitten us on the butt.

Intruding on my thoughts, he said, "I'll let you know when the compulsion has been broken."

"Thanks." I ended the call to find Asa standing on my periphery. "You thinking what I'm thinking?"

"That the director dropped Clay in our laps as a distraction so Bjorn could spirit him away?"

The director knew I couldn't resist an opportunity to save my friend, that trying not to hurt Clay would buy him time to get away. After the wig-tracking-spell fiasco, he was probably glad to be rid of him once he realized we wouldn't give up on him easily.

"Why would Luca free Bjorn?" I drew my knees to my chest. "What good would that do her?"

Had there been more to Clay's warning? Too bad we couldn't wake him up to ask, but the risk of triggering situational orders from the director was too great.

"Bjorn is with the director?"

Jerking my head up, I spotted Colby gliding in for a landing on Asa's head. "We think so."

"He was a prisoner for a while, right?" Her antennae shot upright. "Long enough to leave DNA?"

Witches, and anyone who spent time with them, learned fast not to leave any hair, nail clippings, blood, or saliva where an enemy might find it and use it against them. That, or they died. Often horribly. Bjorn, as close as he stuck to the director, knew better than most to never leave parts of himself behind. But it was a different beast entirely when you were isolated in a cell. Disposal options were more limited, and *no one* would hang around to clean up after themselves in an enemy lair if the cell doors swung open to set them free.

Not even type-A Bjorn. His devotion to the director was borderline obsessive, but he wouldn't have hesitated to book it out of there.

"Yeah." A grin broke across my face, and I sought out Dad. "Can I borrow your magic?"

"Of course." He glanced between Colby and me. "I would be happy to hunt Bjorn down for you."

Poor Dad probably thought this meant I was letting go of the idea of having the other anchors removed. *Nope.* I had just about talked myself into going again, actually. But I was happy to rely on him for spells I couldn't perform for myself at the moment. The rest? Well. He would figure it out soon enough.

CHAPTER NINETEEN

While the black witch began the painful process of removing Isiforos's tattoo, Fergal drove out to where the prisoners of our personal war against the director were being held to collect the material required to track Bjorn. He would be with the director. Of that I had no doubt. The giant had a one-track mind where his master was concerned, which made Bjorn an ideal beacon.

The plan was for Fergal to overnight what we required, which meant we had hours to burn.

Back at the hotel, Colby sat on the couch with the laptop, a frown knitting her brow.

"Find anything else?" I stretched my arms over my head. "Any giant red arrows pointing toward Luca?"

"Most of this information is useless," she admitted. "It's like when Clay and I were gone. You had no clue where we kept the passwords or accounts or anything else. You couldn't use any of the resources issued under your pseudonyms to make tracking your movements harder. You were stuck with the Bureau card or paying out of pocket for any purchases."

Either of those were easy to track for anyone who knew me by Rue Hollis and had the faintest computer skills and access to the Black

Hat database. The Bureau credit card got used anytime I had a big business expense or wanted people within the organization to be able to find me. Like when I showed up to work cases. But I only used my personal debit card at home, in Samford. It would be an absolute last resort for emergency spending before I touched it and allowed the taint of this life to touch the one I left behind.

Nan might have been a *bit* shortsighted with her revenge scheme by cutting Luca off instead of leaving it all in place, giving us the means to track her. That, or it had been a ploy. Maybe Nan wanted us to waste our time cracking her codes instead of doing the legwork required to find Luca before she took her revenge a step too far.

As I thought about it, I began to feel lighter, more certain. "What I'm hearing is, Luca is a sitting duck."

When Nan made the mistake of hacking the Kellies, she allowed Colby to return the favor. Colby had the master list of Luca's aliases, and their attendant credit cards. The primary one had been deactivated after New Orleans, but without Nan to issue new ones, Luca only had those identities to choose from.

"She won't have Nan to cover her tracks," Asa agreed. "Colby can trace her if she uses any of the cards on file."

"And those charges will lead us straight to her." Colby rubbed her hands together. "She's going to make mistakes. We just have to be watching when she does."

Given the maniacal glee in Colby's eyes, I didn't think the watching part would be an issue.

THE PACKAGE FROM FERGAL ARRIVED RIGHT ON SCHEDULE, AND I SET IT in Dad's hands the next morning. He had a few things to prep before starting his spell, and Colby was assisting him by pulling up a map of the US on the tablet he had used for hunting Clay. She could narrow it down once he locked on to Bjorn until he hit on an area.

Bjorn hadn't been free long enough to flee more than a state away.

He faced the same airline woes as Clay. Bjorn was a large man. Hence frost *giant*. The blue thing worked against him too.

As I paced the hotel room, waiting for news, Asa walked in with drinks and food for everyone.

"Can we talk?" He handed the bags off to the wargs, guaranteeing we wouldn't see them anytime soon. "Outside?"

"Yeah." I ignored the foreboding twinge in my gut. "Sure."

He and I exited the room, took the stairs, and found a bench in the empty lobby.

"You're making me nervous." I let him tug me down beside him as he sat. "What's wrong?"

"The centuria needs me." He kept our hands linked. "I have to go to Hael and put an end to this before we can't walk it back." He rolled his thumbs over my knuckles. "I'm sorry, Rue, but I have to think of my people."

They weren't his people anymore, not really, but he had been raised as the high prince of Hael. That didn't just go away because he lost his title. Gave it away, really. For me.

Sending him off with my blessing and support was the least I could do. Even if it made me want to vomit thinking of him going alone.

"What's your plan?" I steeled my spine to avoid wrapping myself around his leg and refusing to let him go unless he dragged me along with him. "How do you see this going?"

"Moran has arranged for a meeting between me and the rebels. I will listen to their concerns, draft a list of their demands, and present it to Calixta."

"You're going to do what now?" The spit dried in my mouth. "She'll kill you for trespassing."

"She needs to secure her kingdom. She believes these rebels are at fault for the unrest." He exhaled. "The truth is, they wouldn't have taken these steps if we hadn't goaded them into it with our actions."

"You know how you're always telling me things aren't my fault? Well, this isn't yours. Not all of it. Carver told us there was a subset of daemons loyal to you. Would they have acted on their beliefs? Maybe.

Maybe not. They might have chosen to sit back, give Calixta enough rope to hang herself, and *then* made their move to dethrone her using her mistakes as their justification."

"I need to do this." He cradled my cheek in his palm. "Our strategy has run its course."

"I'm not going to stop you." I wanted to, but I wouldn't stand in his way. "But I would like you to avoid confronting Calixta until I can pave the way. With her rule under threat, she won't leave Hael. With my ties to you, and my former position as her heir, I doubt she'll let me go to her either. Using a messenger will make our conversation take twice as long, but I'm going to pitch an idea."

"I'm listening."

"To show there are no hard feelings, I could suggest she appoint you ambassador to Hael. Tell her you could bridge the gap between the people of Hael and their former Haelian Seas queen." I rubbed my forehead. "I'll clean up the pitch before I make it, but that's the general idea. What do you think?"

"It's brilliant." His eyes warmed. "It's a position I would be happy to hold indefinitely."

To step back from the throne had given him a minor identity crisis, and I'd thought Black Hat might fill that void. At least for a time. The swiftness with which he accepted my suggestion confirmed his heart might not be set on the throne, but he did care for the denizens of Hael.

Sooner rather than later, I might have to name a new deputy director.

But that was a problem for another day.

"We'll see how it goes." I stood with him when he rose. "Are you leaving now?"

"I need to pack first, but yes. Tiago has offered to escort me."

"Good." I blinked to stop the room from going wobbly. "I'll see if Dad can portal you there."

"Let him work on tracking Bjorn. The sooner we get the director in hand, the quicker we can finish negotiations with Calixta for Aedan. She'll be more tolerant of my interference if she's convinced things are still firmly under her control." He hesitated. "Also consider that if I'm awarded a permanent position in her court, it would allow me to check on him from time to time." His tone softened. "Ten years is a long time to wonder if your cousin is safe."

"Thank you." I couldn't let myself get excited about the idea. It was still a long shot. "You're the best."

When a smile stretched his lips, I couldn't resist tasting it. Heat sparked in my middle when he rewarded me with a groan. But like everything else lately, there was no time.

"I'll write to Calixta." I kissed him again, soft and quick. "Keep your head down until we reach an agreement." I set my hands on his shoulders. "Be ready to run if she refuses to play ball with us."

"I can't run." His eyes held regret but also determination. "I will, however, be careful."

"I'm liking this plan less and less the more you expound on it."

A throat cleared behind me. "The spell is ready."

I pivoted toward Dad, reluctant to release Asa, terrified of him venturing into Hael without an invitation.

"I'll send word as soon as I have news to report." Asa dragged me against his chest, wrapping his arms around me until I felt his heartbeat crushed against mine. "Take care of our girl."

Our girl.

I would have loved him for that alone.

"I will." I swallowed past the lump in my throat. "Take care of you."

With a tender smile, he released me, and I followed Dad, afraid I wouldn't let Asa go if I didn't leave fast.

"He's going to Hael."

"You heard that part, huh?"

"Do you think it's wise?"

"I think it's a terrible idea." I joined him in the suite. "But I also know he needs to do this."

The centuria would keep him safe. Any one of them would lay down their lives to protect him. I just hoped it didn't come to that. I didn't want him to carry that burden.

The kernel of conscience I had been growing over the last year was sprouting tiny little doubts. He wasn't wrong that we caused this current crisis, but I wasn't wrong either. The unrest brewing in Hael, the movement to place one of their own on the throne, was bound to bubble over when Calixta wasn't making much of an effect to embrace Haelian culture.

It just might not have reached a boiling point *quite* so soon if I hadn't lit a bonfire under it.

Things were so much easier back when I didn't care about things like collateral damage. The life of a black witch was simple. They did what they wanted, when they wanted, to whomever they wanted. As long as they got their way, they didn't worry about fallout. Lives were as disposable as used tissues.

The whole being a good person and doing the right thing gig was thankless, stressful, and complicated. It made me want to pull out my hair some days. Most days, really. I had grown a lot since I returned to the Bureau, but I still had a long way to go.

Because deep down, I still tipped the scales toward those I loved and away from the innocents I ought to protect.

"Do you think he'll make a bid for the throne, if it comes down to it?"

The question jolted me out of my thoughts. "Goddess, I hope not."

Unless the only way to restore the equilibrium in Hael was to undo everything we had done…

Nope.

I didn't want to think about it.

In fact, I gave myself permission to ignore it as an early birthday present.

To hold on to my sanity, I pivoted the conversation. "You have a lock on Bjorn?"

"I do." He allowed me the change in topic. "I thought you would want to be present when I begin in case things move quickly." He shot a look behind me. "Are you sure you don't want to go with him?"

Until he mentioned it, I hadn't noticed I was locked in a staring contest with the door separating me from Asa. Asa, who was going to Hael. Where my crackpot grandmother reigned supreme.

"No." I almost choked on the word. "He's got this."

Divide and conquer. That was how successful couples managed dual careers, right? Sure, ours might be a touch more exotic than average, but still. "Give me a minute, okay?"

Alone at the particleboard desk in my room, I cleared my mind of fears and worries as I wrote to Calixta. I took care with my phrasing, wishing Meg could check behind me but knowing I didn't have the time for a consult. Plus, she and Mom already had their hands full. All I could do was pray my offer to loan Asa to her as an ambassador would pique her interest enough to prevent her from harming him if she learned I had let him go on ahead without her blessing.

With that done to the best of my abilities, which wasn't saying much, I called a courier and waited with a stone in my stomach until he arrived to accept his parcel with a guarantee of next day(s) delivery.

For messages crossing realms, that was about as good as it got.

After I tipped the courier, I sought out the others, eager to get moving to block out my fears for Asa.

"I've got the map on standby." Colby stood over the tablet, ready to pinch the screen. "We should be able to narrow it down quicker using this app. There's a better overview of streets too."

While Dad prepped his crystal and began his spell, I hoped this thing with Isiforos was about to turn into a blessing. I didn't want to square off against Bjorn again, but there was no doubt in my mind he could lead us right to the director. Just like last time.

As the crystal swept over the screen, Colby panned out, watching for the first hint of a location.

Within seconds, the point stuck to an area south of here, and Colby used her hands to zoom in until the magic wobbled with uncertainty from the exactness she was attempting to extract from it.

"They're in Sweetwater. Near D Bar D Ranch." Dad kept his hand fisted above the screen. "Three hours or so away."

Derry and Marita had done the bulk of their packing last night, and Colby hadn't been far behind. She didn't have much, just her blanket, the laptop, her phone, her tablet, and...okay. So, the girl didn't travel light. She was a one-woman IT department, so I didn't complain as I shoved my clothes into a duffle.

"Dad?" I waited until he put away his crystal. "Can I talk to you outside?"

A hint of wariness crept into his features. I was certain he could guess what I wanted to ask him.

"You want me to remove another anchor."

Yep.

Right to the point.

"I do." I worried a fingernail. "If something goes wrong for Asa in Hael, I won't wait and hope. I *will* go to him, and I'll need to be able to protect him. Against Calixta and anyone or thing else." I quit before I tore a nail. "Magic would be a big help in that department."

"We don't know for sure what this process is doing to you."

"It's freeing me."

"But at what cost?" He speared me with doubt. "Each time, you require healing."

"I'm aware." I could still taste a faint char in the back of my throat. "I'm also more than willing."

"What about Colby?" His concern tipped over into mine. "Does she experience your pain too?"

"Goddess, no." I barked out a laugh. "I would have never left my house in Samford if she did."

As much as I missed my magic, I didn't need it enough to put Colby through the suffering I had chosen.

"Your mother and I have a lot to learn about the *loinnir* bond."

"You've had familiars." I thought someone had mentioned a cat Mom gave to a friend after the wargs chased it up one too many trees and it scratched out someone's eye. "The bond is like that but more."

"And if you die," he said, eyes boring into me, "the *loinnir* bonded to you also dies."

"Think of this as a controlled burn." I wasn't thrilled with risking her either, but this was bigger than Asa. I was coming unraveled as my magic sought its own way free. "The only way to prevent the wildfire that will sweep through me when your binding fails is to start digging trenches to slow the spread."

"I assume you want me to remove another before we depart?"

"We have a few hours. Marita or Derry can drive to Sweetwater while I recover."

Chin dipping to his chest, Dad gave it a moment of thought. It made me wonder if he struggled for the right answer as often as me. He was a better man because of Mom's influence, but it wasn't the same for people like us. She was innately good, like Colby, while he and I had to stop and think first. Always.

The more I did the right thing, the easier it got. Well. Sort of. More like I was training my brain to react a certain way to a series of stimuli. It would become instinct, eventually. I hoped. If you considered a thing that had to be taught instinctual.

Resolve lined his face when he lifted his gaze to mine. "Where do you want to do it?"

"Somewhere folks won't hear the screams and call the police."

"All right." He didn't ask me if I was sure, and I appreciated it. "Let the Mayhews know."

A big part of me wanted to text Marita instead and then jump into Dad's arms so he could zip me away from her temper. I didn't want to subject myself to what came next, but no one else had any bright ideas on how to remove the Hunk. And I wanted more than to remove it.

I wanted to destroy it. I wanted the Maudit Grimoire to cease existing. I wanted to ruin it the same way it had tried to ruin me.

But first, I had to pay for every drop of magic it had lent me with the pain of revoking its hold over me.

CHAPTER TWENTY

*T*hanks to my Tinkkit engagement ring, whose gift was sending me off to sleep with a twist of the band, I didn't so much as twitch until we arrived in Sweetwater. I can't say that I woke refreshed and ready to face the day, but I was determined and eager to kick frost giant butt.

"I hope you enjoyed your nap." Marita, with Colby on her head, turned in her seat to look at me. "Colby and I could have used another backup singer, but we let you sleep out of the kindness of our hearts."

"Thanks?" I shoved into an upright position. "Has Dad narrowed things down for us?"

"The hair he was using melted." Derry pulled onto the side of the road. "It was ice, I guess?"

The intensity of Dad's focus, paired with the multiple attempts required to track as Bjorn moved, meant he had forced a lot of magic through it. There was nothing for it. We would have to find another way if Dad struck out.

"I'm not sure." I hadn't gotten close enough to Bjorn to tell. "Dad might have zapped it too hard."

The soles of my shoes sank into soggy grass when I stepped out to join Dad, who set his hands on my shoulders to hold me still while he scanned me for any aftereffects from the third and fourth anchors he ripped out of me prior to us leaving Dallas.

I was halfway to the finish line. More than. Closer to freedom from the Hunk than I had been since the day the book fell into my hands. But I knew better than to think the rest would come easily. The price of such magic was never cheap, and I had run up quite the tab.

"Well, Doc?" I forced a smile for him. "Will I live?"

"Yes." His expression cleared, but he didn't smile back. "How do you feel?"

"Sore and weirdly tingly." I shook out my hands. "I'm not sure if it's from Colby healing me—" which she had insisted on doing afterward, "—or if it's a side effect of expelling dark magic from my soul."

No matter how you sliced it, that was what the Hunk had done. Gone straight for the core of my magic. I should have noticed quicker, should have stopped sooner, but looking back I had no idea what I could have done differently.

Sometimes life throws so much at you all at once the only thing you can do is hunker down and pray you survive it.

On the other hand, even though life gave you no pointers ahead of time, you got hit with the guilt, the remorse, the wishing things had gone differently.

Life was kind of a dick.

"The ranch is about a mile ahead." Marita rolled her shoulders, then twisted her torso from left to right, loosening up for the shift after a long ride. She pivoted, sniffing the air, then pointed. "That way."

"Are we driving or walking?" I was stiff from lying boneless across the backseat. "I'm good either way."

"Walking." Derry cracked his neck. "Your dad told us to stop when you woke, so it worked out well."

"I can fly ahead and scout," Colby volunteered, rocketing into the air to burn off her pent-up energy.

"No," we all yelled at once, the volume startling a squeak out of her.

"We don't know for certain the director doesn't know about you." I had a gut feeling Clay had kept his mouth shut, but I couldn't risk it. "The director knows Dad can fly. There might be traps if he's trying to protect himself against an aerial attack. I'm guessing anything that would catch a black witch would work well on magic moths too."

"Oh." She spun into a tight circle, landing on my shoulder. "That would be bad."

"Very bad." I kissed the top of her head. "You can be my parrot, though."

"I'm a captain, not a parrot."

"A captain?" Dad's interest perked. "What sort of captain?"

Ditching me, Colby leapt to Dad's shoulder and began filling his head with stories of the Mystic Seas. The way his eyes lit up when she moved on to the original Mystic Realms, with battles and orcs and strategy, made me think I had lost another person to what I was fast beginning to think of as the Mystic Cult.

Then again, I could see the two of them bonding over virtual bloodshed. It might be good for them.

Content to let Dad watch over her, I trailed after Marita and Derry, absorbing the sights.

The ranch reminded me a bit of the farm outside Samford and sent a pang of homesickness through me that was quickly swallowed by dread. The brief memory of the farm put me in the frame of mind to think on the centuria. That, of course, forced me to acknowledge Asa was absent from his place beside me. He was in Hael. Where Calixta ruled with impunity. And I hadn't heard from either of them.

A cool breeze stirred my hair, drawing me out of my thoughts. The bite of frost hit me next in a shivering wave, and dread punched me in the gut. Bjorn—freaking Bjorn—shimmered into existence barely a yard from where I stood, stinking like black magic. His power hammered at me, icing me to the spot, slowly freezing me in place.

We had been tracking him, sure, but it was out of character for him to engage rather than evade.

"Get her out of here," I snapped at Dad, who had tensed to intervene.

Denial parted his lips, but one look at my determination to save her snapped his mouth shut.

Burdened with the favor I asked of him, he cradled Colby against his chest and flew with her to safety.

Marita slammed into Bjorn in the next breath, Derry right behind her. The frost giant stumbled back, but he caught his balance and swatted Marita's next lunge. He landed a punishing blow to Derry's ribs, but it didn't keep him down. Not with Bjorn advancing on me, the snarl twisting his blue lips promising I would pay for locking him in that cell. Maybe even for daring to exist.

"You can't know how long I've waited for this moment." Bjorn zeroed in on me, which suited me fine. He would kill the Mayhews without blinking, but me... I might retain enough value to the director to survive. I was happy to take one for the team to keep them breathing. "Your days have been numbered since you arrived at the manor, and your ticket has finally been punched."

I told myself I had a pithy comment ready to throw at him, but I couldn't unclench my frozen jaw.

"Stop," Marita slurred, blood running down her chin. "Or I'll make you stop."

Derry took his cue from her, the Mayhews forming a wall in front of me.

No, no, no.

I wanted to yell at them to go, to run, to save themselves, but I couldn't get out the words.

"Just like your mother," Bjorn sneered. "Cavorting with beasts."

"Watch yourself, Frosty." Marita, wobbly on her legs, tensed to strike. "That's my best friend you're talking about."

"Tell your *friend* I don't converse with animals." Bjorn never broke eye contact with me as he flung out his hands to either side. First Derry and then Marita went stiff as he froze them, the same as me. "As loath as I am to touch you, abomination, it's time for us to go."

With careless shoves, he knocked them over, and they thumped onto the dirt. Paralyzed. Magic locking their muscles. But that wasn't the worst of it. No. Icicles grew from his palms. He broke one with a snap, bent down, and thrust it through Marita's chest, pinning her to the ground. He did the same with Derry. There was nothing they could do. Nothing *I* could do as twin crimson stains spread across the soil.

"Interesting." Bjorn peered down at me. "You didn't cast a single spell."

I promised his death with my glare and vowed I would be the one who ended him.

"You're planning something. I can see it. I would kill you and be done with it if it were up to me."

Back at you, I thought, fury boiling within me.

And then the ice encasing me began to melt.

CHAPTER TWENTY-ONE

I thought it was Colby, channeling magic into me across the growing distance between us, thawing me from the inside out. But the burn was familiar. Magic—*my* magic—ignited my veins, engulfing me as it fought the spell Dad had cast to contain my power.

Pain ripped me in two, so much worse than removing the anchors, but the agony was cauterizing.

I overflowed with magic, every cell of my body drinking the energy down like I was a plant and power was rain in a desert.

This wasn't going to end well.

Not for Bjorn. Not for me. Probably not for Colby.

As the Hunk began to radiate heat, begging me to call on it, I found it was easier to block out its siren song of endless power. Dad had torn out the deepest, worst, most festering anchors binding me to it. His spell, which had suffocated the spark out of me in order to save my life—my sanity—had eroded to nothing.

"You're a snotty bastard," I growled, "and you're going to die for this."

Bjorn, who had been bragging about how easily he contained me, recoiled from what he read on my face. He didn't take a step back. He didn't show fear lightly. But the slight shift of his weight was enough for me to grin as I broke his icy hold and punched out, gripping his throat in my hand.

"Where is he?" I channeled power down my arm, zapping him until his teeth rattled. "Where. Is. He?"

I didn't have to name him. There was only one person Bjorn would protect above his own life.

"I'll die before I betray him," Bjorn gasped, and his spittle pelted my hand like hail.

"I was hoping you would say that." I placed my other hand over his heart, reached down deep within myself, and threw every ounce of magic I possessed into that shriveled placeholder of an organ. "I'm not making the same mistake twice."

Thrashing and spasming, the frost giant seized under my hand, but I showed him no mercy. He frothed at the mouth, his eyes rolling back, and then he hit his knees. But I was there, following him down. I kept my hold on him until I hurt, until I ached, until I *burned*. Then I kept on until his ice cube heart fell silent.

His body slumped sideways, hitting the ground, but I didn't let go. I summoned the spell I had used a million times to immolate bodies and reduced him to ash I mixed with dirt to make sure he was dead and gone and never coming back for us again.

Slowly, I crawled toward Marita and Derry, until I knelt between them.

They were dying.

Both of them.

They were my friends.

Both of them.

I couldn't save only one. The other would never forgive me.

Kneeling between them, I fisted the icicles in each of their chests and melted them. With the obstruction gone, blood gushed from the wounds as I planted a palm over each of their hearts and prayed for the power to heal them.

A whiff of rot tickled my nose, a subtle reminder I had all the power I needed if I would just let it in.

No. I aimed the rebuke inward, at the Hunk. *You're the reason I'm in this situation.*

The dark artifact didn't have to respond for me to sense its amusement. I knew as well as it did we were in this together. Our greed for *more, more, more* had forged it. I had let it seduce me the first time, told myself I had no other choice, but there was no going back if I used it as a crutch again. It would own me. Right down to my soul.

The temptation to embrace its power was worse than the craving for hearts had been. I was an addict in every sense of the word. I kept bouncing from addiction to addiction to addiction. Maybe that was my luck. Or maybe it was time I stopped letting life happen to me and started happening to it.

I could do this, maybe not alone, but with help from Colby. Not the book. Never again from the book.

Faint sparkles shimmered under my skin, a glittering warmth that brought tears to my eyes. This was the essence of Colby. Goodness. Love. Kindness. Her magic swirled with it, and as it washed through me, the ironclad grip of the Hunk loosened another degree. As her concentration increased, a brilliant light burst from my pores, funneling through me and down into the wargs' chests.

Derry and Marita began glowing. Brighter and brighter. Until it hurt to look straight at them.

Their wounds sealed, leaving tender pink skin, but their chests didn't rise. Their hearts didn't beat. Neither of them moved.

"Wake up, wake up, wake up." I sank deeper within myself. "I'm not quitting on you guys."

It would be so easy to save them, a conniving voice whispered in my head. *Let me help you.*

No. I held tight to my convictions, but goddess it hurt. *I won't lean on you again.*

We shall see.

As if the surface tension of a bubble had burst, the Hunk retreated, but that wasn't far enough. I wanted it gone. Not hidden. Not protected. Not plotting its next move. *Gone.* Out of me. For good.

Welcoming Colby's power on full blast, I let it surge within me, hot and pure and bright, clearing my senses.

Magic—*my* magic—hit me with the force of a runaway train, and I staggered to regain my balance. Power saturated me from my skin down to the bone and deeper still.

From the start, the Hunk had been holding me back. It had tricked me into believing I needed it by weakening me. Then it fed me what it had stolen in the form of a boost it took credit for.

All the times I thought I required its help was a scam. All along, it had been strangling me, convincing me I was weak. It had been in my head, playing off my insecurities. And if I hadn't been cut off from my magic, if I hadn't felt the difference as it coursed through me, if Dad hadn't pried the Hunk's grip loose, I might have never realized the con job it was running on me until it was too late.

With that realization, as quick as my anger flared, it extinguished.

I don't need you. I never *needed you. Thanks for showing me that.*

Lightning charred my veins, igniting tiny fires within me until I coughed ashes, and the world spun in dizzying circles.

From a great distance, Marita rasped, "Rue?"

I opened my mouth, but all that came out was smoke.

WARMTH FLOODED MY CHEST, AND A TINY VOICE KEPT CHANTING MY name like a prayer.

I was tired. So tired. So very tired.

But I was lighter than I ever had been.

"Her eyelids are twitching."

"She's breathing again."

"I hear her heartbeat."

A punishing *crack* lit up the left side of my face, and my eyes sprung open to find Marita leaning over me with her hand cocked. The persistent throbbing in my cheek led me to believe this wasn't the first time she had tried using tough love to rouse me from…

"What happened?" I worked my jaw and winced from the ache. "How many times did you hit me?"

"The number isn't as important as the result," she hedged, "and the result speaks for itself."

It all came back to me in a rush.

Bjorn. Their injuries. The Hunk.

Gratitude burning in my chest, I flung myself at Marita. "You're alive."

"*You're* alive." She held on tight. "I wasn't sure there for a minute."

What she was saying finally permeated the fog, and ice clinked in my veins. "Colby?"

"Right here." Her voice came from behind me. "Do you think you can maybe help me?"

Slowly, I levered myself into a seated position and angled myself toward her. "What do you…?"

The scene before me made no sense.

None.

Colby sat in the dirt. A small dome of her magic wavered in the air behind her. Within the dome lay a molten glob of metal with a ruby in its center.

"It can't be." I reached for my throat, and my fingers brushed tender skin. "It's gone?"

I traced my neck, marveling over this new sense of weightlessness, a relief so profound I lacked words to describe it. I was free.

Free.

"You had a seizure," Colby explained softly. "I did too."

"You started glowing—and screaming—and the Hunk melted across your chest. I pried it off and flung it on the ground, and it burned the hell out of me." Marita held up her hands to show me her blistered fingertips. "Colby came out of it first, and she rushed to contain the Hunk while Derry started chest compressions to get you breathing again."

"We were about to ask Colby to drop her ward and shift her focus to healing you." Derry ruffled his hair. "Thank God, you woke up before we had to make that call."

Examining the Hunk from where I sat, I couldn't believe it. "The pendant is…"

"Amoebic?" Colby suggested, her voice brighter. "It reminds me of melted ice cream."

"Yes."

"We need to go after Saint." Marita drew my attention. "As soon as you can stand, we're moving out."

"Dad?" A pang hit me in the center of my chest. "What happened to Dad?"

"He got stuck." Colby's wings drooped. "He freed me, but he couldn't free himself."

Murky thoughts churned as I tried catching up to them. "Stuck?"

"A spell." Her voice wobbled. "It grabbed him like fly paper."

I wished I could summon Mom, ask her for his location, if he was okay, but summonings only worked on vengeful spirits. Not *loinnirs* or familiars.

"Since Frosty the Snowgiant was the welcoming committee, I'm guessing this means the director has Saint." Marita wet her lips. "He can't turn Saint, right? Because that would be bad."

"No." I hesitated, a nebulous worry nagging at me. "Dad is the better witch."

Narrowing her eyes on me, Marita rubbed her arms. "That pause concerns me."

"I'm trying not to get ahead of myself." I dipped my chin. "We don't know if it's the director who has him."

"Do you think Luca has figured out Nan is dead?"

"As heavily as she relied on her? Yeah. It's safe to assume she knows."

Maybe not that Nan was dead but that she wasn't coming back.

"Then it makes sense," Derry reasoned, "that Luca would consider accelerating her timetable."

"The director is the point of all this," Marita countered. "Would Luca still even want your dad?"

There was a debt there. We all knew it. Maybe she decided it had finally come due.

If the director had captured Dad, I had a few options. Trades he might consider. Emphasis on *might*.

If Luca held Dad captive, I had a problem. I had nothing to offer her. Nothing she wanted.

Nothing except…

Back when I had assumed the Maudit Grimoire was the Proctor Grimoire, it had been a hot commodity among the rogue black witches who were loyal to Luca. But had it been a reward she offered her faithful? Or had she wanted it and been willing to give them something of equal value if they brought it to her?

After the grimoire became the Hunk, even Dad hadn't known when he was in the grimoire's presence. He, of all people, should have sensed his own creation. But he hadn't. Not until Lake Pontchartrain and the coven it decimated the first time it took control of me.

Perhaps that was why the rogues had finally quit trying to steal it from me. They couldn't sense it either. Its magical signature had become too muddled by the other components to track it singularly.

But how had Luca learned of the book's existence? Its ties to Dad? Its value to the director?

Had she questioned Dad while he was delirious with hunger and thirst? While whatever spell or charm or curse kept Dad docile and his magic contained? Under normal circumstances, I doubt anyone could break him, but after spending decades in the dark, with his father twisting his mind, he could have been driven mad with grief and fury when they first met.

That could mean she was not only aware the grimoire existed, but she knew through a firsthand accounting by one of the authors exactly what filled those pages. Maybe having such a powerful witch —one capable of casting any of the spells in the book that caught her fancy—was Dad's true value to her.

Maybe the vow was simply what she asked for in return because she knew it was what he wanted too. To kill his father. And when that was done, she would set him to her true purpose. There had to be one. All of this couldn't have been for nothing but spite and vengeance. No one was that petty, right?

"Rue, we need you to weigh in here." Marita squeezed my shoulder, helping anchor me. "What do we do with the Hunk?"

"I would suggest a pickup," Derry said, shaking his head, "but it's too dangerous for our courier."

The pendant was no more, the grimoire trapped within a molten cage. But what to do with the cage? The book was clever and wicked, and I had no doubt it would figure a way out eventually. To destroy it was the goal, but I was starting to believe that wasn't possible. For now, containment would have to do.

"I agree." I didn't want to admit he was right, but I wasn't going to endanger anyone else. "I'll carry it."

"No." Marita yanked me back so fast, I almost tipped over again. "You're not touching that thing."

"We'll take turns carrying it." Derry smoothed his hands down the sides of his legs, like he was searching for his pockets. "Anybody got a donation to wrap it in? We shouldn't let it touch our skin."

"What if you need to shift?" I shook my head. "We might need both of you on four legs for where we're going. If you change on reflex, you'll drop the Hunk where anyone can pick it up and use it against us."

"I'll carry it." Colby fluffed out her fuzz. "I'm not afraid."

"Sweetie," I began, but determination radiated off her.

"I can do this. I *want* to do this."

I hadn't been the only one burned by the Hunk. Its insidious tendrils had wormed into her through our bond and caused her to almost kill Moran's son, Peleg, while the kids had been playing. She had as much reason as I did to hate it, and her innate goodness repelled most forms of dark magic. With the Hunk not touching me, our connection broken, she ought to be safe. But *ought to* was a loaded phrase when it came to the Hunk.

"The second you hear a voice or sense anything out of the ordinary, you tell me."

"I will." Her antennae stood on end, her chest puffing out. "I won't let you down."

"You couldn't even if you tried." I ignored the prick of tears in my eyes. "I'm going to cloak you so no one can see you." I almost wept with relief when magic leapt into my fingertips, eager to be spent. "The spell might not stick to the Hunk. With you carrying it, the spell might slide off both of you."

The mass wasn't something she could carry in hairbow mode. She was too small for the weight. Even cat-sized, she would strain under the burden. But I could see how much she needed to do this. How much she wanted to face her fears that the Hunk would ensnare her again and drag her down with it.

Gripping the hem of my tee, I ripped a thick band off the end, leaving me in a stomach-baring crop top.

"Okay." Lowering her ward, she hesitated only long enough to size up before knotting the Hunk in a sling with the fabric. She looped it over her head, wiped her hands, and lifted off. "Here we go."

Once she got within range, I drew my wand and tapped her on the shoulder, casting the concealment.

"Can you see me?" Dust stirred in front of me, and wind kissed my cheeks. "How about now?"

I had no trouble picturing her doing loop-the-loops in front of my face, probably sticking out her tongue.

"Just stay close and be ready to run if you—or the Hunk—are in danger."

With a small gust of air, she rose to—I hoped—an approved height. "Okay."

Losing sight of her, even when she was *right there*, made me nauseous after I had just gotten her back. It didn't help knowing she was giving the Hunk a lift. All I needed was for a black witch loyal to the director to sense it and attempt to shoot her down to claim it.

Not for the director. For themselves. Which might prove even worse, since it would place the Hunk back in circulation. Its iron will would guarantee that. It would bounce from witch to witch until it found someone as easily stamped with *SUCKER* on their forehead as I had been.

After sparing one last glance for the scorched earth where Bjorn had breathed his last, I broke into a run, following beneath Colby as she retraced Dad's flight path.

"Here," Colby announced fifteen minutes later. "It was right about here."

"Hmm." I spun a circle, searching for signs of spells with my vision slightly out of focus. "Are you sure?"

"Yeah." Her voice came from directly above me. "I can smell it."

The wargs fanned out, searching for clues beneath what had been an airborne trap.

"Can you pinpoint the origin?"

The question was a habit born from hanging out with daemons and wargs, but Colby surprised me when a soft breeze whipped past. "The scent trail is…I don't know…trapped?"

"The spell burned out, so I can't see it either." I exhaled. "It left no visible traces."

"You'll have to use your wings and let me show you where I found it."

A prickle of magic stung my spine, and black-tipped silver wings fanned out to either side of me.

For a second, I thought I smelled hydrangeas. A whiff of the magic I had inherited from Mom. One the Hunk had been choking out of me like it had two palms wrapped around my throat.

After lifting off, I followed Colby's voice high into the fouled air, but there was nothing to see. No reason for the smell. No clue what caused it. And no indication Dad had ever been there.

CHAPTER TWENTY-TWO

With all leads exhausted, and the scent trail lost, Colby and I rendezvoused with the Mayhews.

There was only one thing left I could think to try, and no one would be happy about it.

"Colby." I braced for her reaction. "I think I should attempt to summon the book."

"That sounds like a bad idea."

She was right to worry I might want it back for the wrong reasons. She was right to fear what could happen if I touched it again. She was right for holding back, forcing me to think rather than grab after power. But it wasn't the power I wanted this time.

"If we're dealing with the director, and he sees the grimoire, he'll come running."

That book was the biggest enticement I could offer him to free Dad.

"As far as we know, Luca doesn't care about it." Colby stood firm on her No-Hunk-for-Rue policy, which was fair. "We've got a fifty-fifty shot at guessing if the director or Luca captured Saint but a one hundred percent certainty the Hunk will reattach to you if it gets the chance."

A chuff from Marita let me know she was in camp No-Hunk-for-Rue too, but the book was all I had to barter, and the pendant had only ever answered to me. I wasn't sure it could respond to anyone now. The gold was melted, the Tinkkit choker encased in metal. Both of them might be ruined.

The book, and its horrors, might be trapped within it. Forever. Which, I had to admit, was both inconvenient at the present moment and the best possible outcome for the future.

A flash of lightning struck the earth three yards from my toe, and I whirled, bracing for an attack.

The four of us huddled together, ready to face what came next as a flare of brilliance curved into a circle that spun jagged forks until they smoothed into a mirrorlike shine. From the electric frame stepped Asa.

"Asa," Colby trilled, her excitement a soft breeze in my face. "You're back."

"I am," he confirmed, searching for her while scanning our surroundings.

I didn't think.

I ran.

I smacked into his chest so hard, he gasped on impact and stumbled, almost tipping back into the portal.

The only thing that saved us from a return trip to Hael was Moran catching him and shoving him forward to make room as she and six members of the centuria emerged behind him. No friendly neighborhood assassin, but Carver was his own keeper. If he felt he best served me by remaining in Hael, that was what he would do.

"You're okay." I breathed him in, smelling smoke, sweat, and copper. "When I didn't hear anything…"

Time moved differently between this world and the realms you could access from here. Faerie and Hael kept a pretty similar timeline, relative to Earth anyway. Never had I been more grateful for a quirk than I was now, holding him in my arms so much sooner than I ever could have dreamed possible.

"I'm fine." He rubbed his cheek against mine. "Goddess, I missed you."

"I missed you too." I clung to him. "Oh." I winced. "Colby is cloaked, so keep an eye out for her."

"He can't keep an eye out for me." She cackled with delight. "I'm *invisible.*"

"Okay, InvisiMoth, dial it down a few notches."

"Catch me up to speed." He gestured for the centuria to fall back, but Moran held her ground, her gaze a drill that bored into the side of my head. "What do you need us to do?"

Abandoning her taunting of Asa, Colby sat on my head while we got down to business.

"Hael." I forced myself to prioritize his priorities. "Is everything settled there?"

"Far from it." He flashed his teeth. "We've ended the bloodshed—"

"There's always bloodshed in Hael," Moran cut in quick, her mood grim, her eyes sharp on me.

I was definitely picking up on a vibe. Asa must have broken the news to her about Clay while they were in Hael. That look promised things wouldn't end well for me if we didn't awaken him soon.

"We've ended the bloodshed our actions set into motion." He waited a beat to see if she disagreed then continued his update. "Your letter convinced Calixta she requires help to smooth over the rocky start to her reign if she wants to avoid a civil war. She allowed me to assist her with the uprisings, but she made it clear my position is temporary. We've made progress in opening lines of communication between her and her more vocal subjects, which is a good place to begin fixing the division in Hael."

"She spoke to you?" A sour taste flooded my mouth. "I never received an answer either way."

"She sent word to my estate, figuring the time difference would be kinder to me than to you."

As much as it chilled me that she cut me out of the loop, she wasn't wrong in that skipping the middleman was faster.

"He's established a tentative peace," Moran told me with pride. "He would have been a great high king."

For a fraction of a second, I couldn't tell if she was hinting he ought to side with the revolutionaries and take back the throne or if she was merely bragging on him.

"But I understand," she said, after noticing the flinch I couldn't hide fast enough, "why he made his choices."

That was as close to condonement as I was likely to get from her, given her and her people had been raised to serve him as the future king. They would have directly benefited from his leadership, and I was costing them the opportunity for prosperity.

"Even a temporary position means I'll be spending more time in Hael," he warned me. "It's the only way to keep either side from back-sliding."

"I understand." I placed my hand over his heart. "I'm happy to loan you out as atonement."

Maybe it would alleviate his guilt and grant him insight into how he could best aid his people outside the hierarchy. The truth was kings spent most of their lives wrapped in red tape so tight it cut off circulation. Asa was more likely to affect positive change working in the shadows than perched on the throne.

"Your turn." He covered my fingers with his. "What have I missed?"

Since the update was longwinded, we walked as we talked, mostly to burn off my frantic energy.

"You're not touching the Hunk," he said, command heavy in his tone from his time spent with the centuria. "Never again will I risk you to its false promises."

Had I been able to see Colby, I had no doubt she would have been gloating right beside him.

"Now that you're back…" I twisted my fingers in his shirt. "I was hoping Blay could try his luck tracking Dad."

"He's welcome to try." He released me and stepped back. "How are you getting him up there?"

"I'm working on that part." I gave him room as flame erupted at his feet, licking up his calves then higher, until it consumed him. "Hey, Blay."

The crimson daemon blinked away his disorientation, locked eyes with me, and bellowed, *"Rue."*

Scooping me off my feet, he twirled me in a circle at arm's length until I turned green, then hugged me until my spine popped to do a chiropractor proud. He smashed kisses across my cheek and slung me like a rag doll, side to side, my legs swinging until I worried one might fly off and smack Marita in the face.

"I need your help, big guy." I wriggled until he set me down. "We need to find Dad. Fast. Are you game?"

"Blay try." He drew a deep breath into his lungs. "Smell black magic, but not Rue's dad."

"How far can you jump?" Colby sounded thoughtful. "Maybe you could pick up the trail that way."

"Blay try." He crouched down and sprung up higher than I would have expected for his size. He gulped in air then hit the dirt with a shake of his head. "Blay not smell Rue's dad."

"Do you think you could airlift him?" Marita stepped up next to me. "Just a few feet, right?"

"I'm not sure, but I can try." I cast the spell to bring out my wings again. "Hold real still, okay, Blay?"

He made one eager hop then raised his arms for me to clasp forearms with him.

"Here goes nothing." I launched myself, circled around, and locked onto him. "Nothing's happening."

Try as I might, I couldn't budge him. He was too big. I couldn't lift so much as his toe off the ground.

"Blay bunny?" His eye brightened. "Blay cute bunny."

"I don't know the spell," I confessed. "Transfiguration is tricky unless you've got a blueprint."

More so if you were already a shifter, which Asa and Blay weren't technically, but still. Better safe than sorry when it came to magic that altered the fundamental makeup of a person.

"What about levitation?" Derry rubbed his jaw. "That's a thing, isn't it?"

"Yeah." I landed, shook out my wings, then switched gears. "But it can go sideways fast."

"What about that game?" Marita snapped her fingers. "Light as a feather, stiff as a board."

"I don't know what game that is, but it does give me an idea." I turned to the Mayhews. "Got a rope?"

Marita snorted, and Derry cupped his dangly bits.

"Oh. Yeah." I cleared my throat. "You're both naked."

Constant exposure to their nudity made it register less and less when they didn't have clothes on. I wasn't sure if that was a good thing or a bad one, but oh well. Every friendship had its obstacles.

"We'll have to try this another way." I raked my fingers through Blay's hair, fisting my hand in the ends. "I'm going to make you light as a feather." I made sure I held his attention. "You can't fly, not on your own, but I can lift you." I tugged his hair for emphasis. "If I let go, you could get blown away on a breeze. Make sure you stick close."

Bouncing on the balls of his feet, he clapped his hands. "Blay ready to fly."

"You can't fly," I repeated myself to break through his excitement. "Just hold still, and I'll direct you."

"Okay." He did his best to appear solemn, but he couldn't hide his smile. "Blay ready for upsies."

This had Bad Idea written all over it. In bold letters. In Sharpie.

And I didn't just mean Marita teaching Blay *upsies* was a thing.

Careful to maintain my hold on him, I cast the spell and tapped his chest. I let magic sink into his bones, pneumatizing them, filling them with hollows like a bird then whittling his weight down to nothing.

"Blay not-fly now?" He stuck out his arms and flapped them, which sent his hair blowing. "Blay fly!"

The motion was enough to lift his feet off the ground. The slight breeze probably helped. I reached out, let a single finger touch his hip, and watched him drift higher and sideways on an unseen air current.

"Wow." Colby slid down to perch on my neck. "That's a neat trick."

"It's dangerous." I called my wings, and the gust as they settled was enough to send Blay fluttering. "See what I mean?" Had I not been holding on to him, he would have blown away. "Let's get this done so I can return him to normal."

As gently as I could, I took off, dragging him with me. The faint path I carved through the air whipped him like a banner behind me as I returned to the point with the strongest concentration of magic for him to sample.

"You doing okay?" I watched as he sailed like a pennant. "I'm not hurting you?"

"Blay have fun." He grinned wide. "Light as feather." He tucked in his arms. "Stiff as board."

"Mmm-hmm." I let him enjoy himself while I pinpointed a likely spot. "Okay, time to get serious."

Chest expanding, he breathed in until he couldn't anymore, then exhaled slowly, his nose scrunching.

Crossing my fingers, I braced myself to ask, "Can you tell if Dad was here?"

"Spell too large. Just one big stink." He kept sampling the air. "Blay not smell Rue's dad."

"Okay." I deflated on the spot. "Thanks for trying."

That was when I noticed Colby, meaning her cloak had failed. The spell had reached its limits, or it had been sloughed off when we flew through the magic residue. Either way, I couldn't get it to stick again.

Maybe I could convince her to surrender the Hunk to Blay for a while.

"Blay find black magic," he promised, grinning when he noticed Colby. "Find Rue's dad too."

"I know you'll do your best, big guy."

"Blay promise Rue, and Blay always keeps promise."

"Hold on." I tugged him closer. "We're going down."

"Aww." He pouted up at me. "Blay not want to go down."

"Do you want to take over an important job for Colby?"

"Blay help Rue?"

"It would be a *huge* help to me."

"What Rue need from Blay?"

"Colby, pass him the Hunk." I held us steady while she offered it to him. "Let him carry it for a while."

"Keep it safe." I watched him tuck it into his pants. "Don't drop it."

"Blay keep safe." He patted his pocket. "Hunk not escape Blay."

Sucker that I was, I did a couple of wide loops, really dragging out the landing.

The smile stretching his cheeks when I set him down, and only then broke the spell, was worth a detour.

"Upsies." Marita stretched out her arms over her head, wiggling her fingers at me. "Upsies."

"No." Derry made grabby hands at me. "I want upsies."

"No upsies." I scrubbed a hand down my face. "We need to find Dad, then we'll goof off."

Pinky at the ready, Marita stuck out her hand. "Promise?"

"Promise." I hooked my finger around hers and then Derry's. "You'll both get to be light as feathers."

"I can handle the stiff as a board part on my own," he whispered to a giggling Marita.

"Rue, come this way." Blay waved us on, grinning when Colby landed on his head. "Blay smell magic."

Happy to lead the way, we let him play guide across the rocky terrain. Every so often, we paused for him to reorient himself, and I seized the opportunity to scan above us and ahead of us for signs of any traps.

We couldn't very well save the day if we got stuck the same as Dad.

"His nose is better than mine," Derry lamented an hour later. "I don't smell a thing."

"He got firsthand exposure." Marita patted his shoulder. "That's why he can trace it."

"I don't get it." Derry wouldn't let it go. "It should have settled on the ground by now."

I was betting the spell snared Dad, held him aloft, and never let his feet touch down. I was also willing to bet a secondary spell had been cast to prevent anyone walking under it from noticing it had been there.

"There's some weird divide." I joined in to soothe his ego. "Magic is to blame, not your nose."

"Makes sense to come at him from the air." Derry tipped his head back. "Your dad is an excellent flier."

The wing spell was a true work of art, which was why the director had bartered my promotion to deputy director in exchange for it. His envy of Dad's talents knew no bounds, making it more ironic that our current strife with Luca *and* Calixta had been born from his desire to cement his legacy with a child of his bloodline. Only to discover he was unable to parent without a jealous heart.

All the heartaches, the betrayals, the children who never lived to inevitably disappoint him, had been for nothing.

"What's that?" Derry, his vision sharper than mine, picked up his pace. "Is that…?"

Several yards away, a heap of clothing lay crumpled like a wad of paper that missed the wastebasket.

"Dad." I left them behind and ran straight for him. "Hold on. I'm coming. Just hold on."

CHAPTER TWENTY-THREE

$\mathcal{I}$ smacked into a clear barrier as hard as glass, bounced off it, and landed on my butt. Reaching out, I had a second to feel my way up the smooth edges of the containment spell before it hit me I was alone. I got to my feet, turned back the way I had come, and found Marita and Derry collapsed near where they first spotted Dad. Blay was curled on his side in the dirt not far from them, and Colby drooped in his hair.

As soon as I had ranged ahead of them, a spell must have caught them.

That couldn't be a coincidence.

"You killed Bjorn Johansen."

Glancing over my shoulder, I watched as the air beside Dad rippled like a fingertip poking a calm pond, and a familiar strawberry blonde emerged from behind an illusion spell so seamless I had to admire it.

Luca.

Reality shivered a second time, and the director joined her. He wore his company suit, leaned his weight on his cane, and stared off into the middle distance. His expression was serene, and that peaceful façade sat wrong on his features. The man was never happy, never content. He was always grasping, plotting, reaching for *more, more, more*. More power, more influence, more control.

"I did." I got chills when the director didn't so much as blink. "I'd be lying if I said I hadn't dreamed of it for years."

Luca bobbed a shoulder, as if to say fair is fair, but the director appeared to be off in his own little world.

"Do you know how many decades it took me to win Bjorn to my cause?"

A lick of ice swept down my spine, casting refracted images that showed me the last few months in a different light.

"Bjorn worked for you?" I couldn't believe it. "*Bjorn?* Frost giant with an icicle up his butt? That Bjorn?"

"No one was closer to Albert. He was a necessary ally."

"That's how they escaped the explosion." I finally understood how they had known the precise moment to flee. "You tipped off Bjorn, and he got them out of there."

"All it took was Bjorn telling Albert your father had come for his head. Then he became *very* cooperative and more than willing to let Bjorn shepherd him out of harm's way. He trusted Bjorn fully. That was his mistake. In thinking anyone bound into service against their will can ever be loyal. Time hadn't dulled the edges of Bjorn's hatred. It honed it to a razor's edge. One all too willing to cut Albert's throat given half a chance."

"Let me guess. You gave him that."

"Bjorn was a frost giant. A soldier. A conqueror. Your grandfather reduced him to a dancing monkey."

"I, for one, never saw him dance. But it seems like you were pulling his strings just as hard."

"All I had to do was set him free. The rest? He viewed it as a debt of honor I was happy to collect."

"If Bjorn was working with you, why didn't you snatch the director up in Florida?"

The frost giant had hidden the director away in a cabin on Lake Okeechobee, but we hadn't seen signs of Luca.

"Albert was no use to me half dead. For what I have in mind, I wanted him hale and hearty."

"You don't think you're going a *tad* overboard with your vendetta?" I kept a wary eye on the director, whose soulless gaze was giving me heebie-jeebies. "Why not kill him and be done with it?"

"Death is too quick, too easy. To destroy a person, you start at the top and work your way down. To the roots. You rip them out, burn them to ash, then salt the earth so that nothing will ever grow there again."

"How thorough of you."

"You came barreling after me to save your father," she mused, "but not your grandfather."

"You're a smart woman." I returned her earlier shrug. "You know the director's not worth my tears."

"He wasn't always like this." She swept her gaze over him. "He was kind, once. He loved me."

"He loved what you could give him," I corrected her, "right up until you couldn't."

Fae fertility rates were abysmal, and children were rare, but Luca had been born a Guardian of Ish'ran. Her god—also known as Earl—granted each of his guardians one female child in exchange for a single coupling with their counterpart, a Brother of E'rin't. But the director had seduced Luca into bearing his children, and her god wasn't happy about it. He refused to bless their union, and none of their children survived more than a handful of days. When it became clear she couldn't give him the heirs he craved, he left her without looking back to pursue Calixta in the hopes of producing a daemon/black witch child.

"You spoke with Mother, I see." She curled her upper lip. "I should have let the compound crush you."

"Probably," I agreed, checking on Blay from the corner of my eye. "Why didn't you?"

"Your father bound me." She looked puzzled. "He didn't tell you?" She cocked her head. "I can't lay a hand on you. Otherwise, we wouldn't be having this conversation." She chuckled then. "Perhaps he can't recall. His mind was a twisted spiral when I found him. All he did was weep for his wife and his daughter. Frankly, I wasn't impressed with him. I was certain I had to be wrong. That he couldn't have been the one child strong enough to have survived while my babies died in their cradles."

"Love isn't a weakness."

"You didn't used to believe that." She flicked Blay a glance. "You might disbelieve it again in the future."

"That sounds like a threat."

"I thought about adopting you."

"What?" The abrupt change of topic made my head spin. "I did *not* hear you right."

"You were a beautiful child. Talented. Malleable." A gleam lit her eyes. "Desperate for love."

Culture shock had been leaving a home with parents who lavished me with affection for the sterile manor and a grandfather I didn't know, whose sole objective was to hammer me into a shape that pleased him.

"What stopped you? The story I killed my own parents with reckless juvenile magic?"

"I let myself imagine what it might be like, to raise you in my image." Her smile turned cruel. "Then to show Albert the girl who had been meant as a reflection of him had turned into a mirror of me." She exhaled. "But then I saw in you the same core of determination that had begun to wither in your father, and I accepted that you would become a casualty, the same as my children had been."

"Plus, I'm a blood relative." As much as it shamed me to admit it. "Your salting of the earth philosophy requires my death."

"That too." Her gaze slid to the director. "I don't mind him, when he's like this."

"Under your thumb? A veritable zombie? A shell under your absolute control?"

"Yes," she hissed, her eyes narrowing to slits.

"It sounds like you're the one desperate for love."

A bark of laughter twisted her features, draining them of any real amusement. "I don't need love."

"Says the woman who enslaved her former lover."

"He's the second most powerful witch alive," she ground out between clenched teeth. "He will help me tear down the foundations of his legacy. He will bear witness to his own destruction. He will watch as I wipe his bloodline from the face of the Earth, destroying his hopes as he ruined mine." Vindication gave her a dewy glow. "This time, I was more cautious. This time, I will succeed in bringing him to his knees."

"This time?" I studied her. "This is your second attempt?" I don't know why it popped in my head, unless I had been worrying it in the back of my mind since Mom became a vengeful spirit. "The Boo Brothers?"

"They taught me subtlety was lost on Albert," she said darkly. "That a full-scale assault was the only hope I had of gaining and holding his attention."

"How much of your treasure trove did you steal from Black Hat's own vaults?"

Her cunning smile was answer enough, and her confession explained how she came into possession of a shard like the ones the Amherst siblings had used to conceal their black magic nature. It had been hers before she passed it on to the Boo Brothers in what must have been her inaugural attempt at taking down the Bureau.

A prickling sensation tingled down my nape, jarring a thought free that hadn't occurred to me sooner.

The director had likely cast the spell that trapped Dad. Only a strong witch could have tricked him. But someone had cast the spell on the director, and it wasn't her. She was fae. Her powers didn't work that way, or she wouldn't have had to fake her heritage to blend in with black witches. That meant she had one more accomplice nearby. One powerful enough, or familiar enough, to get close and cast a spell to rob the director of his autonomy before he could deflect the attack.

"Who else is here?" I kept my gaze locked on her. "You couldn't have done this on your own."

"An old friend." A slow smile spread her red lips. "I believe you two know one another."

Kenneth Cale, a black witch from the Lyonne coven out of Beverly, Massachusetts, appeared next to her. I shouldn't have been surprised to see him again. He was her current lover and the one responsible for the compulsion tattoo on Isiforos.

"No hard feelings, I hope."

"None whatsoever." I tipped my chin. "As soon as I kill you for what you did to Isiforos, we're square."

Chuckling, he summoned a foul wind that sent my hair swirling around my face, blinding me.

Before I could wipe my eyes clear, I hit my stomach, clipping my jaw on the ground, and spat dirt.

He had moved quicker than my eyes could track. No wonder he had gotten the drop on the director.

He drove an elbow into my spine, shocking a gasp out of me. As soon as his weight left me, I torqued my hips, flipping onto my back, but he stood a foot away. I couldn't reach him. I had to lure him in. Only one way to do that, and it would hurt. A lot.

"Come a little closer," I wheezed, locking my arms down at my sides, leaving my tender middle exposed. "Let's see you laugh in my face."

Without flinching, he kicked me in the gut and then in the chest before zipping back to a safe distance.

He was fast. I couldn't do faster. But I could be prepared for his next strike.

Spitting blood, I wedged my elbows under me. "That all you got?"

With a smirk, he delivered a punishing kick to the underside of my jaw that left me seeing stars as my skull bounced off the ground. I didn't have to fake my disorientation as I let my head loll and my eyes spin from the brute force of his attack. I breathed through clenched teeth, every inhale whistling as my aching ribs protested the motion.

Kenneth crouched to drink me in, the big bad director knocked on her butt, and couldn't resist getting in a parting shot while I played possum. He fisted my hair, yanking me to him, putting us nose to nose.

Big mistake.

Only a matter of time before he made one.

He really shouldn't have held on. I had him now. He was done.

Funneling magic to the point where our skin met, I sent him flying. His limbs seized on impact, jerking, and his facial muscles spasmed as his scream morphed into pathetic whimpers. His head tipped to one side, tears and drool wetting his cheeks. Eyelids twitching, he quit moving. Alive, based on the rise and fall of his chest, but probably wishing he wasn't. I had hit him with the equivalent of a taser powered by a lightning strike.

An arched eyebrow was all the sympathy his predicament elicited from his lover.

"Hiding anyone else?" I breathed through the white-hot pain in my side. "Any other surprises?"

"Just this one."

Dad rose from his limp sprawl with the same dead-eyed stare as the director.

Beside him stood...my mom.

Just as lost as he.

"One moment." Luca stepped behind the director, murmured to Dad, and Dad bound his father's wrists at his spine. He then cast a spell that brought life surging back into the director's gaze. "There."

As the director's expression cleared, it darkened with the promise of retribution, but that was what brought us here. He wasn't going to scrape together enough hate on the spot to beat Luca at her own game.

"How dare you?" The director gnashed his teeth at her. "Our business has long been done."

"We're done when I say we're done." Luca gripped his jaw in her hand and jerked his head toward me. "I want you to see this." She snapped her fingers at the end of Dad's nose. "Kill her."

Manic laughter poured from the director as he watched the unfolding spectacle.

"You think I care about her?" He laughed louder. "Or him?"

Hard to keep an ear cocked to their conversation with Dad striding toward me with my death in his eyes.

"They are your legacy." Luca, clearly put out by our dysfunctional family, forced him to watch. "Your line ends with them. Your only living child, and your only living grandchild, dead. You've already lost your compound, your fortress. Soon, you will lose the secrecy shrouding our world from humans, and with it, any leverage to rebuild your precious Bureau. The new world will have no need for the old rules, or for those who enforce them. You're no better than a common thug selling protection to those who only need to be kept safe from *you*."

"You don't have to do this." His jaw flexed with the effort of civility. "We can start over." He softened his gaze on her with such precision it was clear to me—if not to her—he had plenty of practice. "Together."

To make sure he didn't escape this unscathed, I reminded her, "He *left* you."

Mom drifted behind Dad like a shadow. She didn't blink or talk. She simply existed next to him.

As much as I hated that she was, yet again, reduced to a pawn, I was grateful she wasn't fighting me.

A few feet away, Dad drew his wand, cocked his arm, and flung a spell at me.

I yelped as I dodged the blast, having forgotten he was able to lob power without the book.

I could almost hear the Maudit Grimoire's seductive whisper.

Use me. Bond with me. Be mine, and I'll always be yours.

"No," I growled under my breath. "You don't get to win. You don't get to take up space in my head, book. Not anymore. I'm done with doubting myself, and I'm done with you."

Wielding his wand like a blade, Dad sliced through the air above me.

I dodged his swing. Okay. Fine. I tripped and stumbled out of his way.

Not fast enough.

A hank of my hair drifted past the end of my nose where the blade of magic had caught it.

Dad advanced on me, cutting off my escape with blasts of power that herded me where he wanted me. I led him farther from Blay and Colby, and the Mayhews, trying to protect them, but he was too fast. I couldn't touch him to cast on him, and the only way that would change was if…

No.

No, no, no.

The Hunk was not an option. The Maudit Grimoire was not a savior. They couldn't do this for me.

I had to save myself.

A blue streak dried the spit from my mouth as Mom broke from her stasis.

This was about to get ugly.

Summoning my wings, I prepared for takeoff, but suddenly she was there.

Right in front of me.

What do I do? What do I do? What do I do?

Hurt one, I hurt the other. Kill one, I killed them both.

How did we all get out of this alive?

"Circle back, baby." Her eyes were wide…and clear. Had she been playing along? Did that mean Dad was okay too? I couldn't tell, and I couldn't afford to guess wrong. "Run toward Luca."

"Mom?"

The second of connection came and went too fast for me to second-guess her. I did what she told me. I spun on my heel, praying this wasn't a trick. I aimed for Luca, bobbing and weaving to obscure the method to my madness.

"I hope you know what you're doing," I muttered to myself, evading Mom as she herded me with feints.

As we drew closer to Luca, she shifted her weight, eyeing us with burgeoning concern.

Beside her, the director had begun to smile, and it was an ugly thing.

Sharp. Predatory. Knowing.

Just before I would have bowled Luca over, I cut left. But Dad kept going. He collided with her, knocking her back, and he rode her down. He landed on top of her, and quicker than she could order the director to help, he drew his athame and stabbed her through the heart.

"This…isn't…over…" Her lips trembled. "The humans…"

Blood slid from one corner of her mouth, and her body trembled with her struggle to hold on to life.

"Allow me to return to my post," the director said to Dad, a gleam in his eyes. "I can set things back to rights. All can be as it was before."

The way he didn't look at Luca, even for a second, made me furious for his role in this all over again. That disregard of her, of her feelings, had led us here. His heartlessness had cost countless innocent lives, and he had the nerve to ask us to raise him back to a position of power.

"You're dead." I limped closer, my calf muscle twinging. "You don't get to resurrect."

"I can make it as if none of this happened," he argued. "I can protect humans from—"

"No." Dad reduced Luca to ash he mixed with the soil then rose. "This won't have been for nothing."

"Are you going to kill me?" The director laughed, bitter and hateful. "Your own father?"

"You're safe from me." He had no intentions of invoking the animus vow with Mom by his side and the promise of a future together. "But I'm not the one you should be worried about."

"Her?" He dismissed me the same as he had the day I showed up on his doorstep. "She won't kill me."

"You're right." I cocked my arm and punched him square in the jaw. "I have other plans."

Eyes rolling back in his head, the director hit his knees then fell sideways.

I bent to retrieve his cane and broke it over my knee. The sound was positively liberating. It didn't erase what the director had done to me, the wounds he had inflicted on me, but it still felt pretty damn good.

"You okay, Dad?" I searched for any signs of lingering influence. "You had me going there for a minute."

"Father couldn't hold me." He made it sound as if I had suggested the sun orbited the Earth. "When I saw Luca had Father in her thrall, I played along. I wanted to be ready to help however I could." He smeared Luca's remains further with his foot. "Without her, we might never uncover all the agents she conscripted or the covens she recruited for her scheme."

Thanks to Nan's final act of defiance, we had a place to start. Besides, it wasn't like folks ended up in Black Hat because they were cute and cuddly. Rebellion wasn't a shocker when they didn't want to join up anyway. I had to work on that. The company-loyalty thing. But it was a low priority currently.

"Without her, the movement to expose humans will die. As it always does." I worked on catching my breath. "The supplies will dry up too."

A low groan drew my attention to where Blay was turning onto his back, clutching his head in his hands. The angle, or his hair, obscured Colby and set my heart racing.

"Oh no," I breathed and rushed to his side, skidding to him on my knees. "Colby?"

"Here." She climbed from under a messy hank of his long hair. "I'm here."

"How are you feeling?" I sat back on my ankles. "How are you *both* feeling?"

Wobbling as she walked onto his shoulder, she decided, "Weird but okay."

"Blay not feel so good. Head hurts. Belly hurts too."

After I helped him sit up, he ducked sideways, startling Colby off him, and dry-heaved until his stomach accepted it was empty.

The Mayhews weren't as lucky. The remnants of the spell caused them to vomit the rather impressive contents of their stomachs. But they were both upright and coherent. That was progress.

"What did we miss?" Marita wiped her mouth on the back of her hand. "I spent the last however long at a disco and missed all the good parts."

"A disco?" Derry frowned. "You saw spinning mirror lights? All I got was strobes."

"Raves suck," she commiserated. "I'm glad we weren't at the same party."

Confused what any of that meant, I let it wash over me as I examined them from where I knelt.

"You're both okay?" I settled back on my ankles. "You weren't hurt?"

"We're fine." Marita flopped down on her back. "I just need a minute."

"Me too." Derry lowered himself beside her. "That was a wild ride."

Flames erupted on my periphery, and I turned back to find Asa returning my assessing glance.

"You're handling this much better than them." I brushed the long hairs from his eyes. "Must be all the portal travel. Your stomach is used to having worlds turned upside down and spun around."

His soft huff of laughter set off another heave, so I nudged him onto his back to recover his equilibrium.

"Are you sure you want to trade him?" Mom stood over the director. "He causes so much trouble…"

"If I can't kill him," Dad countered, his lips pinched, "then neither can you."

"Mom is a white witch." I hardly needed to remind them. "She would never…"

An echo of the vengeful spirit she had been before Dad anchored her to him as a *loinnir* sharpened her features. Okay, so she wasn't the exact same person she had been. But I still didn't think she would kill him.

Though, from the look in her eyes, she would happily stand back and watch me do it.

"We should get him to Calixta." Asa reached out a hand for me. "As quickly as possible."

Linking our fingers, I sat down and thought about the logistics of that. "Did you set up an exchange?"

"She understood the time delay would mean she had to wait. We have two days." He frowned. "Or did."

"Two Hael days or two Earth days?" I bit the inside of my cheek. "Never mind. Stupid question."

Calixta would figure she had waited long enough, and I couldn't blame her for wanting to finish our deal. But this fiasco with Luca had taught me a valuable lesson. I had never been an eager student, but unfortunately for the director, I liked to think I learned from my mistakes.

CHAPTER TWENTY-FOUR

*A*sa and I stood on the shore below the ruined cliffside where the compound once perched like a vulture over the sea. How many times had the director gazed out his window at the ocean and reminisced? The compound, in hindsight, not only connected him to Luca, but Calixta as well. He had given no thought or care for Luca. Had he ever thought about the mother of his only surviving child? Of what he had done to her? How he had treated her? What it got him in the end?

A son who hated him.

A granddaughter who despised him.

No legacy. No dynasty. No nothing.

"Are you ready for this?" Asa kept his head forward, gaze cast across the sea. "After this...it's over."

Overhead, Dad pinwheeled, keeping watch over me while distancing himself from the scene.

"Don't get ahead of yourself," I cautioned him. "It won't be over for ten more years."

Until Aedan walked out of the sea, I wouldn't consider this deal with Calixta done.

Even then, we might never fully cut ties with her or her court if Asa continued to offer his services.

A churning of the waters announced her arrival. A dozen sharks, mostly tigers, splashed their long tails in the shallows. Tentacles longer than I was tall rose from the deep, waving like strands of kelp in a current. At the center of that pageantry, standing on the creature's forehead, stood Calixta. Draped in a severe gown of inky black fabric, its hem spilling into the water in rippling eddies, she greeted us with a frown.

"You have something that belongs to me."

That was it. Straight to the point. As if the last few days hadn't happened.

Did she know we were behind the uprising? She probably had her suspicions. She had sat on the Haelian Seas throne long enough to have a keen eye for machinations. But she wanted the director enough to go along with the deal as if this had always been the plan.

"I have the contract ready for you to peruse." I held it out over the water, and a sharp-toothed fish leapt to snatch it out of my hand. "As soon as we've both signed it, I'm ready to fulfill my end of the bargain."

"Rennet." She snapped her fingers, and a skeletal man with splotchy grayish skin covered in scales stuck his head above the water. "See that the paperwork is in order."

The fish zipped it to him, and he patted it on the head as he took the scroll and unrolled it.

Time spent waterproofing the paper and ink had definitely not been time wasted the way he kept dunking it as he bobbed on the waves.

Asa and I stood in the sand for more than an hour while he read the contract, pausing to cast a gimlet eye at me, but he did finish eventually.

"The document is sound, my queen." He presented the paper to Calixta with a low bow. "You may sign, if it pleases you."

"A moment." Calixta put him off while she pretended to consider me. "You sent a letter, pleading with me to award your mate a position of authority within my court."

Pleading was a strong word, though I would have if she had pressed the matter.

"Your court was in turmoil." I studied her right back. "We offered you a boon."

"Hmm." She inclined her head. "The timing was convenient, yes?"

"That we reached you before any real harm was done? Yes. The goddess clearly favors you."

"As soon as I gave you a deadline, I found myself unable to leave my realm. Unless I sent my heir in my stead, which is not without its own complications." A knowing look glinted in her eyes as a smile played on her lips. "You could have been magnificent, you know. As my heir. Your mate would have made a fine consort. He would have paved your way with his people the same as he's paving mine."

Hmm.

Calixta had mellowed toward us since our last meeting, which caused the hairs to stand up on my nape. She was giving me too much credit for his ideas. Asa was the one who understood Hael, and its politics, well enough to manipulate them. Not me. I was just along for the ride.

"I appreciate the vote of confidence, in both of us." I inclined my head. "But that's not our path to walk."

"You've decided it's not for your cousin either." She scoffed. "Is a throne so uncomfortable?"

For Asa? Yes. For me? Definitely yes. For Aedan? Absolutely yes.

"You sit the throne well." Asa pressed a hand to his chest in a neat bow. "Better than my father did."

That wasn't saying much, in my opinion, but she savored the flattery, and so I kept my mouth shut.

Before Calixta switched gears, which was starting to sound like she knew what we had done and wanted compensation for it in some form, I shot the text to Fergal to present our trade then I turned to watch.

Behind us, high on the cliff, the vampire walked the director to the edge.

A quiver started in the director's knees and rose into his shoulders as he beheld his fate, squirming like a worm on a hook. He didn't attempt to make nice or spout *what might have beens* at Calixta.

Luca had taken the long view. She had been willing to dedicate her life to destroying his. He must have read weakness in the way she circled him for so long, deciding on a course of action, debating what fate he deserved, getting as close as she dared to him.

Had I given him to her, she might have forgotten her reasons for hating him. Eventually. If he played the role of repentant lover well enough. She might have even forgiven him. In time. A mistake that would have cost Luca her life.

Maybe that was why, despite her exceptional planning and the chaos she achieved, she had been too tied up in her own revenge to make good use of her resources. She could have done so much more, so much *worse*, but her tunnel vision had been her downfall.

Calixta, on the other hand, hadn't been willing to give him that much power over her ever again. If I hadn't dangled him in front of her, tempted her, she might not have gotten around to considering her revenge for decades. Not until after she had been High Queen of Hael long enough to grow bored with her contentment and turn her head toward fresh entertainment.

But in gifting him to her, I had given her the best of both worlds. She could pursue her own agendas, and in her downtime, savor every second of his ruin in payment for the throne and life and son he had stolen from her.

"I have a knife handy if you need one." I held up the athame Dad had offered me earlier, then reminded her, "The contract must be signed in blood for the binding to activate."

Her tongue darted out to wipe her lips, and her teeth glinted as she smiled up at the director.

Revenge so close, she could taste it, made all the sweeter by his dawning horror.

She stuck out her hand, Rennet placed a blade carved from a spiral shell on her palm, and she sliced her fingertip. She signed a sloppy X, big and bold, ignoring the sharks frothing the surf to taste each crimson drip spilled until the cut sealed itself. She tossed the curling paper to Rennet, who swam it over to us.

The icy chill of his skin brushed me as I accepted and cut my own finger with the athame. I used a sigil to represent myself, one that also powered the magic licking across the paper, turning the ink golden.

"The bargain has been sealed," I announced, the weight of the last few days lifting. "We are in accord." I gestured to Fergal. "Bring the prisoner."

I watched as the director entered the lift, as the platform lowered him down the cliffside, as he took his first step onto sand toward his new reality. He speared me with a look that bordered on pleading, but he stiffened his trembling jaw when he read the remote disinterest on my face. "Any last words?"

"I still control the golem." He straightened his shoulders. "He will never be free of me."

You will never be free of me was what he meant, and somehow I managed to hate him a little bit more. I would never give up on Clay. He knew that. Knew I loved Clay too much to cast him aside. Even after this latest fiasco, it didn't change how I felt about him. None of it was his fault, so how could I blame him?

The director wanted his memory hanging over our heads, clouding our future, obscuring our plans.

But I was tired of that, tired of him, tired of cleaning up after his messes and paying for his crimes.

"Funny thing I learned about golems during all the years I spent attempting to free Clay from your influence. If their master has no power—specifically, no magic—they have no way to control them. It's required to maintain the bond between master and servant." I noted the slip of his certainty. "I didn't think much about it. It was good to know but ultimately worthless information. As long as you lived in the compound, surrounded by agents, you were safe. I couldn't touch you."

A crinkle of worry pleated his brow as he began to tally up the sum of what I was telling him.

"I'm wearing anti-magic cuffs," he said slowly, trying to convince himself. "Your father put them on me."

While Luca had amassed an impressive trove of magical toys, the cuffs were standard Bureau issue.

"Hmm." I leaned in, lowered my voice. "No." I savored the drain of color from his cheeks. "You're not."

"But I don't feel…" He swallowed hard. "You *didn't*." His breaths turned choppy. "You *couldn't*."

"Dad spent a long time down in the dark with nothing to occupy his mind but revenge." I almost laughed at his utter shock. "Do you honestly think you weren't the target of those fantasies? That he didn't keep his heart pumping by imagining all the ways he would destroy you after he walked free?"

A bare whisper made it past his lips. "No."

"You took what he loved from him, and he spent that time crafting a binding spell to take what you love from you: your magic. He could have bound your power well enough on his own, but we made it a family affair. I offered up my blood too. Now it's a familial binding."

The director made noises that never gained enough traction to form words.

"You'll never cast another spell again. You're going to Calixta's court powerless. And when I wake Clay, he's going to be a free man. You'll have no control over him. Not unless we decide to give it back. And I think we all know that's never happening."

The director gaped at us then staggered back, bumping into Fergal. "*No.*"

"Yes." I gripped one of his arms, and Asa took the other. "Allow us to escort you."

Digging in his heels, the director fought to break free, but we didn't give him an inch of wiggle room as we walked him into his future.

"Here you go, Grandmother." I was careful to keep my shoes out of the water. "I hope you enjoy your new toy."

"She tricked you," he screamed at Calixta. "They've bound my power. I'm no use to you like this."

"This is my second boon," I told her, backing away from the surf.

"That's no boon," he snarled at me. "It's…it's…"

"No worse than you deserve."

If possible, Calixta's smile grew wider. "I accept this, your second gift, and square our debt."

The squid shot out a tentacle, wrapping it around his torso, and yanked him under the water.

"I almost forgot." I held up the key to the standard handcuffs. "You might need these."

"What for?" Calixta's smile glittered with malice. "He'll grow used to the weight of chains soon enough."

"Oh." I slipped it back in my pocket. "Well then."

"You will come with your mate," she decreed with imperious certainty her word would be law. "You will attend me while he is fulfilling his duties among the people."

About to tell her, in very colorful language, how that was never going to happen, she held up a hand.

"Do this, humor me, and I will allow you to see your cousin during those times."

"Do you mean see him as he walks past me in the hall? Sits across a crowded room? I need specifics."

"It would seem my graciousness knows no bounds." She heaved a sigh. "You will be given six hours once per month. Not one second longer. If you fail to show, we will hunt you." She lifted her hand, palm out. I couldn't discern the mark of our original binding, but I knew a threat when I saw one. She was showing me she had the means to track me through that old link. "If you outstay your welcome, we will slit your throats and feed your corpses to the crabs."

"Rats?" I offered, reminding her she was the monarch of Hael and not its seas.

"Rats," she agreed with a wrinkle of her nose. "Land creatures are so hairy and inelegant."

I didn't see much difference between a crab picking flesh from my bones versus a rat gnawing it off, but I wasn't going to antagonize her. Not when this was going so well. And certainly not when I was, apparently, going to see her once a month until she terminated Asa's position.

Sand flew as Dad struck the beach in a crouch with the force of a punch. "I will accompany her."

"You don't trust me with your daughter," she surmised, her expression sour. "You…care for her."

"I love her," he corrected her, his attention touching on the spot where the director had vanished. "I was given more of a chance to know her than you were to know me, but Father cost us both something precious." He rested his hand on my shoulder. "I lost her once. I won't risk her again."

"You may enjoy safe passage as well," she said after a long consideration. "However, if you—or your daughter—seek to liberate Albert Nádasdy, say in ten years' time, your lives are forfeit."

"I give you my word I have no interest in my father or his fate or his future."

"Me neither," I chimed in quick, happy to reassure her he was one gift we didn't require a receipt for.

As she began sinking into the water, Dad and I stood shoulder-to-shoulder and watched until she and her retinue had returned to the depths.

"Quality family time." I cocked an eyebrow at him. "I didn't see that coming."

"I don't like how much she praised your ruthlessness." He shook his head. "It was too admiring."

"That's what worried you? I was more afraid she would attempt to trade for Asa."

Had she known the extent of his influence, she might have decided ruling Hael would be easier with the former high prince on a smaller and lower throne beside her.

"She will require an heir when Aedan is released from his duties. If she gets you under her sway, she might not look any farther for his replacement. She's cunning, and neither of us can afford to forget it."

Because I was curious and had recently undergone my own parental-identity crises, I asked, "No interest in fostering a relationship with your mother?"

"I regret what Father did to her, to us, but no. I'm not opposed to developing a cordial relationship with her, but I'm not interested in inviting her deeper into our lives until she proves herself trustworthy."

So, sometime next to never then.

"I can respect that." I let my head fall back on my shoulders. "I can't believe we actually did it."

"We secured Aedan's freedom," Asa said from behind me, "but we have more work to do if we intend to stop what Luca put into motion."

"You're right." As ready as I was to set down my burdens, it wasn't time yet. "Everyone, pack for Boston."

With access to Nan's files, Colby could track down Luca's remaining allies and their stashes of king killer. From there, the Kellies could coordinate efforts with agents in the field. But first, we had a stop to make.

CHAPTER TWENTY-FIVE

*J*siforos sat in a cell playing solitaire on his bunk with a deck that looked as beat up as I felt. He heard the door open at the end of the hall and lifted his head with resignation in his eyes. He spotted me, and the cards fell out of his hands.

"Hey." I waved to him, like an idiot. "Ready to get out of here?"

Jumping to his feet, he gripped the bars. "Are you serious?"

"Luca is dead." I winced at the scar tissue left from his tattoo removal. "You're free, in more ways than one."

His forehead hit the metal, and his fists tightened, but he couldn't bring himself to look at me again.

"I'm sorry, Rue." He blew out a long sigh. "I'm so damn sorry. For everything. I know that's not enough. If you want to demote me, kill me, or revoke your licensing permissions with Dad, I understand."

That he lumped the loss of his dad's crafting empire in with his death as potential punishments told me I wasn't wrong. He was one of the good ones.

"You don't owe me any apologies. You were under orders. You had no control over yourself or your actions. You never would have done the things you did without someone else forcing your hand."

The clench of his fingers lessened, but he didn't withdraw. "But—"

"But nothing." I was a pro at this, having given the speech to Clay many times. "You're absolved of any and all wrongdoing. The tattoo is gone. Even if someone from the Lyonne coven tried to use it to control you, they can't." I covered his hand with mine. "It's okay, Isiforos." I pried each digit off the bars. "Let's go."

When he finally hauled his gaze up to mine, his eyes shimmered. "Where to, boss?"

"The hotel. We need to coordinate with the Kellies."

His swallow was audible.

"They know you're not to blame." I hooked my lips up in a grin. "However, I would recommend taking Arthur a tumbler of fresh, body temperature blood and Kelly some Kung Pao chicken with a quart of hot and sour soup. Apologies always go down easier with food. Not that *I* think you need to make nice, but I can't speak for them. Plus, it never hurts to bribe the folks in charge of case assignments."

A guard arrived a few minutes later and let Isiforos out.

I walked him through the building, to the curb, and put him in a waiting SUV.

"Clean up, eat something, rest." I smiled. "Then get your butt back in black and to The Spinnaker."

We had a lot of work to do.

THE PINE CRATE STOOD THREE FEET TALLER THAN ME AND FOUR FEET wider, and the only thing that kept me from ripping the door off with magic and flinging it was the fact Clay didn't need to breathe to survive stasis. Still, it caused my heart to beat harder to find him trapped in an airless box. Even if he didn't know, I did.

The location I chose for this awakening was strategic. We were out in the middle of nowhere. Nothing in sight but grass, grass, and more grass. A sea of the stuff. It was serene, in its way. Isolating too.

Clay would have no choice but to listen to us if he wanted a ride home. That, or he could ignore us for the half day's walk to the nearest town. I was hoping, with Colby present, her face wet with tears, he would see reason. But, I had to admit, that was also what worried me. The tears.

"I brought crowbars." Derry handed one to each of us. "Let's get him out of there."

Marita, Blay, and I put our backs into prying off the front while Colby flew loops over the top.

"Are you sure he's okay in there?" She held a stylus in her hands. "He's not…?"

She would have chewed her fingernails to the quick if she had any.

"He's okay." I said it as much for my benefit as hers. "I promise."

Wood splintered as we gained leverage, and a cold sweat drenched my spine. A tiny gap was all we needed for Derry and Blay to slide their fingers in. They pried off the front and tossed it aside, then each took one of Clay's elbows and lifted him out of the box.

The second he touched down, Colby plastered herself to his scalp, sobbing her heart out.

"We'll take care of the mess." Marita clamped a hand on my shoulder. "You take care of him."

As the Mayhews carried off the crate to return to their storage courier, Blay and I got comfortable.

"Rue pet." He offered me a length of his hair. "Pets make Rue feel better."

"Mmm-hmm." I rolled my eyes. "I'm sure it will."

While I played the role of the sucker I was, Colby got to work redrawing Clay's *shem* with exquisite care.

"Here we go," she whispered, finishing the final loop, holding her breath as his innate magic began thawing him. "Please be okay, please be okay, please be okay."

Her chant nearly broke my heart, but the worst was yet to come.

"Hey." He spotted her first. "What's with the tears, Shorty?"

The familiar intonation, the warmth, the *life* was back in his voice.

"Clay." She flung herself against him again and held on with everything in her. "I'm so glad you're back."

That was when he noticed we stood in a field with nothing around us for miles, and his face crumpled as he locked his gaze with mine in a silent question. Always the same one.

What have I done?

In the past, I had hidden episodes from him when I could get away with it to spare him more pain. I couldn't this time. There were too many witnesses, and he would wheedle Colby down until she broke.

"We have a lot to talk about, old friend." I didn't give him a chance to recoil, just slid my arms around him and hugged him close, grateful to have him back. "Want to sit?"

A faint tremor moved through him, warning me he might stagger if he didn't, and he nodded twice.

"Yeah," he rasped, cradling Colby in his hand. "Let's sit."

Scooting me aside, Blay accepted Clay's weight and eased him down gently.

We sat next, careful not to crowd Clay. I rested my hand on his knee as I told him what he'd missed from my point of view. I wished that had been the end of it. I saw in his eyes he did too. Then came the hard part.

While Colby remained in barnacle mode, she began telling her side of the story, and I did too. Both of us afraid of how he would react and what he might do to distance himself from those actions until he could accept them.

"I didn't hurt you?" He held Colby on his palm, level with his eyes. "You're sure?"

"I'm sure." She hugged his thumb until anyone else would have lost circulation. "You took care of me."

"And you let her go." I rubbed his shoulder, having the same problem. "You saved her life."

Familiar with what came next, I prepared my secret weapon.

"I endangered it in the first place—" He spluttered when I launched my attack. "That was my *eye*."

The water gun I had kept concealed was the size of a navel orange, but I had spelled it to never run dry.

"You have two." Colby giggled. "Besides, it's just water."

"Et tu?" He clutched his chest. "I thought you were on my side."

"I am." She drew the tiniest water gun on the market, barely the size of a plump strawberry. "Mostly."

Pulling the trigger, she shot water up his nose, and he coughed until he spat beside him.

"Oops." She cringed. "I didn't factor in the angle."

"Shoot me all you want." He kissed the top of her head. "Drown me if you want. I deserve it."

This time Blay shot him in the ear with his cannon-sized soaker, and he yelped when it hit him.

Did I forget to mention the water was ice cold? As in, fresh glacier-trickle cold?

I mean, if you're going to spell something, you might as well spell it right.

"What was that for?" He scooched farther from us. "I accepted the blame—"

"Exactly." Colby shot him in the cheek, shaking her head all the while. "Quit it."

"No blame," Blay echoed, firing madly, soaking his shirt. "Clay stop or else."

Eyes darting between us, Clay couldn't help but blurt, "But it was my—"

"Hmm?" I shot him in the forehead, my aim getting better all the time. "Did you say something?"

"No." He covered his face with his empty hand. "I didn't say a thing."

Noticing Blay take aim again, I rested my hand on his weapon and forced him to lower it.

"There's one more thing I wanted to tell you." I locked gazes with Clay. "You're free."

"The director is with Calixta." He pieced it together. "He can't get to me unless—"

"There's no *unless*." I gathered his large hands in mine. "No ifs, ands, or buts either."

Confusion charted a course across his features. "I don't understand."

"Dad and I bound the director's magic. He has no control over you."

"Clay do what he wants," Blay explained. "Like Blay."

"That's not possible." His fingers went limp. "A golem always has a master."

"He could walk up to you on the street, beg you to save him from Calixta, and you could tell him no."

"Clay." Colby sailed onto his head and leaned down to put them eye to eye. "You're *free*."

A sob cracked his chest like a boulder splitting. He pressed a hand where his heart ought to beat, but he couldn't hold in the sound. He rocked himself, arms wrapped tight around his middle, while Colby caressed his brow. Tears poured down his cheeks, and he was helpless but to let them fall.

"Come here." I pulled his head down onto my shoulder and rocked with him. "It's going to be okay."

"Am I dreaming?" He hiccuped against my neck. "Is this real?"

"One hundred percent." I kissed his cheek. "You're safe now. You're *you* now. Forever."

"I love you, Dollface. I don't say it half as often as I should, but I do. Thank you."

"It was a group effort. I can't take all the credit." I squeezed him close. "I love you too, you know."

"Yeah, well." Colby dropped a kiss on top of his head then glided over to nuzzle me. "I love you both."

"Blay loves everybody," he announced. "Everybody loves Blay?"

"We love you both too," Clay and I said in tandem, as if we had rehearsed it.

"Good." Colby twitched her wings as her attention snagged on the sky. "Then we should get going."

"Yes," he gusted out, standing in a rush. "Let's go…find a trash can for those guns."

A shadow blotted out the sun, and Clay spun with a clenched fist until he spotted its owner.

"Moran," he breathed, his expression somehow eager and miserable at once.

A stream of water nailed him between the eyes as she came in for a landing, her pistol-sized squirter in hand.

"Not you too?" He groaned as he wiped his face dry. "I thought you were here to save me."

"I am." She shot him again, point-blank. "From yourself."

"That's our cue to leave." I hugged him quick then stepped back, summoning my wings. "Colby?"

Stubbornly, she clung to him. "Do I have to?"

"Yes." I opened the neck of my shirt. "Climb in."

As she sailed over, she shouted, "I love you, Clay."

Bouncing on the balls of his feet, Blay yelled, "Blay loves Clay too."

"Dial it down, you two." I couldn't stop my smile. "We'll see him again in like ten minutes."

As Blay watched Colby disappear, where she settled against my chest and looped her arms through my bra strap, an idea struck him, lighting up his face.

"Upsies." Blay waved his arms over his head. "Blay call upsies."

"Good grief." Clasping hands with him, I cast the spell to make him weightless. "Hold still."

With everyone secure, I launched us into the sky.

THE NEAREST TOWN WAS TINY, WHICH HAD BEEN THE IDEA, AND THE Black Hat SUV idling in the parking lot of a boarded-up fast food restaurant stuck out like a sore thumb. Fergal sat behind the wheel, wrapped up as tight as a mummy. Arden rode shotgun, and she climbed out the second my feet hit the cracked pavement.

"Well?" Her focus slid over my shoulder. "Where is he?"

As soon as I released the spell on Blay, flames engulfed him, returning Asa to me.

"Change of plans." I helped Colby out of my shirt. "He's awake, but…"

"Moran wanted a moment alone with him," Asa finished for me. "She called earlier with the request."

Colby, eager for Clay to return, wasted no time ditching us and gaining altitude for a better vantage. Not that she was likely to catch a glimpse of him, but hope springs eternal.

"She didn't want an audience?" Arden's eyebrows winged higher. "Interesting."

"Their relationship is...complicated." I didn't have a better answer. "I'm trying to stay out of it."

Much like I was a package deal with Colby, Moran had to consider her son, Peleg, in all her decisions.

Things were different now. Clay was free. As free as any golem could hope to be. But she had almost lost her son once, thanks to the Hunk manipulating my bond with Colby, so I wasn't sure it would be enough to convince her he was worth the gamble.

I hoped she would give him a chance, a real one, now that things were as close to normal as they got for people like us. But Clay was notoriously private when it came to his romantic relationships, a luxury he didn't afford the rest of us, so who knew where they stood in the aftermath of...well...everything.

"You've got that look." Her lips pinched. "You want to talk to me about what comes next."

"You need to head back to Samford." I didn't sugarcoat it for her. "The Bureau is no place for humans."

"What do I do with everything I've learned?" She shook her head. "I can't unlearn it."

"I'm not suggesting you do." I had a second, better offer for her. "I'm hoping you'll put your skills and knowledge to use at the farm, with the centuria. It's not far from Samford, so you could live at home. You could keep working at the store and volunteer there in your spare time to keep a hand in."

"A hand in how?"

"Few of the daemons had ever visited this realm until recently, and they could all use help acclimating. To our world, to having a say in their own lives, to living among humans. Who better to help them learn to be more human than a human?"

Her brow gathered while she thought about the offer, and she cut Fergal a glance.

"Moran can take over your training." I sweetened the pot. "I need Fergal, and he wouldn't enjoy country living anyway. He's a big-city vampire."

Most were, really, but only because that made it easier to feed without calling attention to their dining habits.

"Will I see him again?" She scuffed the toe of her sneaker. "He's… grown on me."

For that exact reason, I decided I had been misusing a valuable resource. Fergal was an excellent training officer. He enjoyed mentorship. He was patient, kind, and—most importantly—in control of his impulses. I planned to place my teenage recruits under his care. I believed he would be good for them.

From this point on, he would be in charge of our juvenile recruitment program start to finish.

Until we figured out a better way to handle underage offenders, the kids could use someone like him.

"I can see you two are friends, and I won't stand in the way of that. You can call, email, text, whatever."

"I can visit him?" She rose onto the tips of her toes. "That would be *amazing.*"

Several different warnings rattled around in my brain, but I couldn't shake a single one loose.

"I don't like him like that." She must have read my concern in my face. "He's just really cool."

"You seemed to like him like that plenty not so long ago."

"I might have been curious about sex with a vampire. Who wouldn't be? Seriously? It's so hot when you read about it. But…" She picked at her thumbnail. "Sex isn't a Band-Aid. There are some types of pain it can't heal." She sneaked a glance up at me. "Even if it might be fun trying."

Her laughter at my sharp intake of breath peeled back the layers, the hardness, revealing the girl she used to be. The one who couldn't have survived in our world but was determined to hold her own now.

"I miss him," she confessed softly. "Aedan."

"I do too." I didn't want to have this conversation, but it was happening. "That's why I worry about you."

"Camber swears the quickest way to get over a guy is to get under a new one." She spread her hands. "It seemed like a good idea at the time."

"All bad ideas do."

"I'm glad you stopped me from making a mistake with a person who could be a good friend to me." She exhaled. "He really is fantastic in the ring. I could watch him for hours." She caught my expression and laughed. "Not in a pervy way. I promise. Though have you seen him without a shirt because—"

Sticking my fingers into my ears, I plugged them to avoid hearing about pecs or abs or whatever else.

Finally, she tugged my arm until I let her win and faced her head-on.

"I'll behave." Her grin said otherwise, but I was glad to see it. "And I'll go to the farm. To help however I can." She finally got around to the question I had been expecting from her. "Will you be there?"

"Often if not always." I couldn't say yet where the Bureau, therefore I, would land. "But you can visit me whenever you like." I gave her a stern glare. "As long as you tell everyone where you're going *before* you arrive at the airport next time."

"I will, I will." She studied me. "You look like you've got more to say."

"I wanted to do this when Camber, you, and I could be together." I rubbed the base of my neck. "That's not going to happen for a while. We still have to root out anyone else loyal to Luca and patch up the Bureau's public image." The time for speeches had finally come. *Ugh.* I had avoided addressing our allies for long enough. "We also have to rebuild our headquarters and a million other things."

"You're scaring me."

"I want you and Camber to have my house." I didn't give her a key.

They both already had them. I did, however, buy keychains meant for realtors with tiny houses and even tinier sold signs on them. "I can't live in Samford full-time, and I don't want the house to fall into disrepair waiting on a day that might never come." I pressed the keychains into her palm, but she didn't so much as blink, so I rushed out, "I also want to give you two the shop." Along with whatever kept eating those blasted winter rosebuds. Arden, at least, would be equipped to deal with that now. "You've been running it yourselves for the past year. You've proven you can do it. I don't know if you want—"

Arden flung herself at me, wrapping me in a suffocating hug. "This is too much."

"You've earned it." I hugged her back. "Ten times over."

Guilt was a part of my reasoning, of course, but mostly I just wanted the girls safe and secure without me. A job where they were their own bosses. A home near their parents without a mortgage. I would even throw in my SUV to give Arden her own ride so she and Camber didn't have to share anymore. Those were tools that would help them live full and successful lives.

"If you give us your house—your *house*, Rue—and your shop..." Emotion thickened her voice as she held on tighter. "Will we ever see you?" She hiccupped a sob. "This isn't a trick, is it? It's not goodbye?"

"It's not a trick." I kissed the top of her head the way I did Colby. "It's definitely not goodbye."

"Okay." She sniffled and withdrew, wiping her cheeks with her palms. "Okay."

"You can take a minute." I laughed softly. "You don't have to decide now."

"No one needs a minute to decide that *yes*, they want a free house." A manic laugh escaped, and she slapped a hand over her mouth until she could control herself. "You're setting us up for life. You realize that? We could live in Samford, run your shop, and never want for anything." She sobered. "You're sure this isn't a goodbye? I agree and then never see you again? You're sure? You *promise*?"

"I'll give you a blood vow if it makes you rest easier." I chuckled under my breath. "You're not getting rid of me that easy." I angled down my chin. "Especially now that you know our secrets."

Arms folded across her stomach, she paced from one end of the empty parking slot to the other.

Once, twice, three times.

"You can't do it like this." She lurched to a stop. "You can't dump this in my lap and expect me to explain to Camber... I don't know what I would even say." She tossed the keychains back to me. "Come to Samford, take us out for dinner, and break the news then."

"I don't know what to say either," I confessed, voice tight. "I was hoping you would know."

"We'll figure it out." She released the tension in her shoulders. "We've got time."

For once, we had all the time in the world.

CHAPTER TWENTY-SIX

Four weeks later.

HEAD TIPPED BACK, I WATCHED THE CEILING PINWHEEL ABOVE ME AS I spun circles in my task chair in the Office of the Director at the Black Hat Bureau's official temporary headquarters in Boston, AKA The Spinnaker.

Yes, I bought the hotel. Well, not me personally. Black Hat ponied up the cash.

With the Kellies secure in their ballroom, the database functional, and an okayish relationship with local law enforcement via Captain Peters, Boston was as good a place as any for the Bureau to recover while a new compound was built on top of the bones of the old one. There was nice symbology in that, even if it came with ghosts from our pasts. It helped that the Bureau already owned the property.

Initial estimates for construction were *astronomical*. I had to save money somehow. Using land Dad had inherited upon his father's death, and then deeded to me, made the most sense. Especially after I got an advance viewing of the blueprints Clay had been sketching since his appointment as Director of Fun that included a heated indoor pool, tennis court, basketball court, bowling alley, and home theater.

Eventually, I would have to break the news that I couldn't afford every single thing. That he would have to let a few items slide. More than a few. Most of them had to go. His list was ridiculous.

There was also a rather impressive hole carved into the cliff, right down to the ocean floor, that I had decided would make an ideal tomb for what remained of the Hunk.

The Kellies wouldn't be returning to their former quarters, in case they had other hidey-holes we didn't know about, so I might as well put their hard work to good use. Until we discovered how to destroy the Hunk, if it was even possible, we had to settle for containment.

The plan was to pour a layer of concrete thirty feet deep, toss it in, and then watch it sink while I cackled to do my little moth girl proud. Only once that set would I fill in the other seventy feet until the chamber was full and the book was encased in a solid block that wasn't going anywhere without me knowing about it.

After that, I could ward the whole chamber to hide the molten Hunk's power signature. I planned to hire the water witches who helped us contain Pontchy the sea monster in Lake Pontchartrain to ensure the ocean didn't erode the magic. The cost of their services would trim a little more from Clay's wish list, but the Hunk—the Blob?—was the priority.

For now, I was too grateful to see a bounce in his step again to pick a fight over which ideas got the ax.

"Dollface." Clay stuck his head into the room. "You're going to make yourself sick if you keep going."

"I'm bored." I put my feet down, stopping with him in my sights. "What's taking Asa so long?"

He clamped a hand on the doorframe, and rainbows glinted off the diamond band around his ring finger.

"Put that thing away." I shielded my eyes. "Did Moran have to get you such a huge engagement ring?"

"She's under the impression I'm extra." He twisted his wrist to make the stone glitter. "I have no clue where she got that idea. I'm a simple boy with simple needs."

That private talk between Moran and Clay? Yup. This was the result.

There had been some confusion on her end about traditional gender roles in mixed-species relationships between golems and daemons, but Clay didn't mind one bit. He wanted to be sure she was sure, so their wedding date was set a solid two years away, on his chosen birthday.

That was the excuse he gave when I asked why they had chosen to wait, anyway, but Clay put the *extra* in *extra*vaganza, as Moran clearly knew when she went ring shopping. I figured he needed every second of that time to plan his wedding bash.

Asa and I hadn't set a date yet, but I half expected Clay to hand me an invitation one day out of the blue for my own ceremony. It was a very man of honor/wedding planner thing to do. Factor in Derry as Asa's best man, in charge of the bachelor party, and I was girding my loins a lot lately. That didn't touch on the self-appointed best friend of honor, Marita, who had zero interest in planning a wedding but wanted the final word on the menu as well as a seat at all the tastings and her name added to the gift registry.

Tapping a finger against my chin, I wondered, "Do simple boys have walk-in wig closets?"

"Let's leave my wigs, and any closets they may or may not have, out of this."

"Hey." The angle was hurting my neck, so I sat all the way up to see better. "Have you seen Arden?"

Arden, who made it a month before she got permission from Fergal to come visit, had spent the day as a student. She had sat in on Fergal's inaugural lecture on folklore that was the precursor to the curriculum he was developing for juvenile recruits. She hadn't stopped chattering about it since.

The novelty of a human in class meant questions aplenty from the other students. She had been as thick as thieves with Eliza Toussaint, and her girlfriend, Tibby Garnier, by the time the bell rang. She was in touch with Riley West, Captain Peter's niece, as well. I was glad she was growing her circle of friends but sad she would forever straddle the line of fully belonging in either crowd. Para or human.

"She and Colby were hashing out the playlist the last time I saw them."

Tonight was the first of the Director of Fun's organized events for agents to blow off steam.

"I thought you hired a DJ?"

"I thought I did too, but he didn't show."

"Bummer."

"Yeah, well, the girls will do a better job anyway." He ran a finger along the inside of his shirt collar. "Plus, Colby said she could really use the money when Super Mystics drops next month."

"How sure are you the DJ wasn't cancelled?"

"Rude." Clay slapped a hand across his chest. "What are you accusing Shorty of, exactly?"

"Taking steps to ensure she can afford any add-ons they make available?"

Mounts, clothes, weapons, pets.

Sucker that I was, she had already conned me out of the cost of the expansion pack itself.

"The nerve." He huffed. "I'm offended on her behalf."

Leaning back in my chair, I dug my thumbs into my eyes. "Mmm-hmm."

"You okay there, Dollface?"

"Just tired."

After a month of nonstop travel on the *We're Black Hat, and We're Totally Okay* grand tour that carried Asa and me around to the major cities with a strong Black Hat presence, I was burnt out on socializing. It had been worth it to engender goodwill from the people we worked alongside but also mind-numbing to perform the same song and dance routine in every city to prove the Bureau's solvency.

Watching bad decisions happen in real time wasn't my top pick for how to spend our first night back, but I was the director now. Sacrifices must be made. I could visit the open bar, smile and wave, and then crawl into bed in the penthouse suite that was our home for the next however long it took to rebuild the redesigned compound and the less imposing manor we intended to offer as free housing to agents.

A knock on the wall drew my attention to where Asa stood framed in the doorway.

"Hiya, handsome." I wiggled my fingers at him. "I was starting to think you got lost."

"I'm counting on you, Ace." Clay punched his shoulder. "Get our fearless leader downstairs in five."

"Don't worry." He smiled a small smile. "I'll take care of Rue."

As soon as Clay left, I stood and invited myself into Asa's arms. He stroked my back and kissed my cheek.

"Politicking took its toll on you." He slid his hand under my shirt to tease my waist. "You need to rest."

"As soon as the party is over," I promised him, pleasant warmth unspooling in my middle.

"What if, instead of partying, we pick a vacant room at random and spend the next week naked in bed?"

Heart thumping harder, I rested my palms on his chest, over his heart. "What would we tell Clay?"

"The petting zoo I hired to set up in the parking lot ought to distract him. There are baby goats. He might not even notice we didn't make it. And, if he does, they have ducklings and a wading pool on standby."

Ah. That explained the wait. "And what would we tell everyone else?"

"That the Director of Fun is in charge until we return from a highly classified mission."

"Okay, okay. I see you've thought of everything. But I'll only say yes if you agree to a 40-30-30 split."

Caution won out, and he asked, "What does the 40-30-30 stand for?"

"Forty percent sleep, thirty percent sex, and thirty percent cuddling with movies and takeout."

"How about fifty percent sleep, and we split the other half between sex, movies, and takeout."

"They do say good relationships are about compromise."

"Then pick a number between one hundred and six hundred."

"Two hundred and sixty three."

"Room two hundred and sixty three it is." His fingertips dug into my skin. "Have I told you I love you?"

"Only a few times today. Like five or six." I stuck out my bottom lip. "So, basically, it's been an eternity."

"I love you." He pressed his lips to mine. "More with every—"

A loud pounding noise startled us apart, and we spun to face the door.

"Rue," Clay yelled, proving his timing was as flawless as ever. "I know you and Ace are still in there."

The door was the only exit, and if we walked out it, we wouldn't see the inside of our room for hours.

Or, it *would* have been the only exit, if I wasn't a highly motivated gray witch.

After pressing a finger to my lips, I pointed to the window. I crept over, flipped the latches, then flung it open. As a gust of wind fanned Asa's hair, I climbed out, hanging off the frame, and summoned my wings in a rush of silvery magic.

"I'll give you to the count of three," Clay warned, "then I'm coming in."

Holding out my hand, I waited for Asa to decide. "Do you trust me?"

"You have to ask?"

He slid his palm over mine and up my arm, until our forearms were locked, then he stepped onto the sill.

"*One.*"

I held myself aloft while I cast the *light as a feather* spell over him.

"*Two.*"

Wings pumping, I rose, lifting Asa off his feet while he grinned with the same childlike joy as Blay.

"*Three.*"

A thud echoed behind us, and I shot higher, faster, Asa dangling from our handclasp.

Clay stuck his head out the window as we cleared two more floors.

Whatever threats he shouted at us were absorbed by the traffic, the wind, and Asa's and my laughter.

Our world could be dark and dangerous, cold and uncaring, but as long as we had each other, the ability to laugh at ourselves—and the speed to outrun indignant golems—we could survive anything life threw at us.

But having a petting zoo on speed dial probably didn't hurt.

Aedan

Ten years later...

The house was the same. Small. White. The hill was greener than I remembered, gentler too. I heard the creek running behind the house, its burble a familiar lullaby from my life before.

I was the only thing that had changed, the only thing that no longer belonged, but I had to come.

The driveway might as well have been paved with glue for how my feet stuck now that I was here.

An unexpected guest, I stared and stared, wishing I would catch *her* in one of the windows.

The front door burst open, bouncing off the siding with a suddenness that shot my heart into my throat, but the thin silhouette emerging onto the porch didn't belong to *her*. Or to Camber.

A girl around fifteen locked gazes with me, and tears sprung to her blue eyes. She broke into a smile that caused my ribs to creak under the weight of her stare. She leapt the stairs, hit the grass, and ran straight for me.

"Brother." Elise—sweet little Elise—threw herself at me hard enough to bruise. "You're here."

The last time I saw her, she was five years old and spitting mad at me for handing her over to the cleric. It had taken me six months to convince him to place my much younger siblings into foster care to protect them from our eldest sister's maliciousness. To foster each child in a different family had been my own idea. It tore us apart, and I had been prepared for them to hate me for it, but it had given them the best hope of surviving to adulthood when Delma had wanted to slit all our throats to become Calixta's heir.

"How is this possible?" I wrapped my arms around her, hugging her close. "How are you here?"

"Rue found us." She held on like I would vanish if she took her hands off me. "All of us."

"Rue...found you?" I had been promised that was impossible. "How...?"

"Okay, well, Colby located us. She's the *best*. Then Rue picked us up and brought us back."

Colby.

I should have known.

The last part of Elise's comment stuck with me, and I asked, "You live in Samford now?"

Before Elise could answer, the door flew open again. Three more girls and one boy spilled out in a tangle of limbs. They ranged in age from eleven to seventeen. They spilled down the front steps in a rush of yells and laughter, kicking up gravel as they stampeded toward me.

Impact knocked me to the ground. I landed on top of someone— probably Elise—who yelped before crawling out from under the pile of wriggling and squealing bodies pinning me.

"I missed you."

"Hi."

"I love you."

"It's really you."

The tumble of words scrambled together as my vision blurred, either from sharp elbows and bony knees that kept sinking into my gut or from this unexpected surprise I never could have imagined awaiting me.

A shadow stretched across my face, and the kids scattered, leaving me in a bruised sprawl.

"Sorry about the dogpile." The figure leaned over me. "I swear I warned them to behave."

Her.

It was *her.*

Years ago, I had locked her name in the vault of my mind and thrown away the key. It broke free now, as my vision cleared to find her offering me a hand up before the kids swarmed again.

Arden.

It was *Arden.*

My Arden.

"You know them?" I wiped the sweat off my palms before allowing her to help me to my feet. "How…?"

I wedged my legs under me, but my knees shook. Fear. Excitement. Anxiety. I couldn't tell.

"First things first." Arden took her hand back, leaving my fingers to curl as they chased her warmth. She twisted the inside of her wrist up for me to see then tapped an old scar. "We're going to talk about this."

The courtship mark I left on her the last time I saw her ignited heat under my skin, but she hadn't agreed to bear it. I shouldn't have done it, gifted her with one of my scales, but it had kept me sane knowing she carried some piece of me with her.

"When a girl says that to you, it means you're in trouble," Daniel informed me. "Big trouble."

"You're *really* in fascination with Arden?" Allie bounced on her toes. "Can she *really* be our sister?"

"I can't believe she waited for you." Caressa thinned her lips. "For *ten* years."

The sharpness of her tone told me the waiting hadn't been easy for her either. As the oldest, she carried the most memories of me.

"She could have gotten married and had babies like Auntie

Camber." Talia blinked wide eyes. "Then you would have cried and cried and cried, like that time my toenail fell off after I stubbed my toe on coral."

The idea of Arden marrying someone else carved me hollow, and I caught myself checking her fingers for a wedding band even though Talia said *could have*. Not *did*. But Arden's hands were bare.

"Back to the kitchen, brats." Arden clapped her hands loudly. "Finish icing the cupcakes."

They ducked in, formed a huddle, and hugged me close before scampering back to the house.

Once we were alone, I found the courage to search her—*Arden's*—face for signs I was truly welcome.

"You sound different." She hesitated. "Not in a bad way. Just more formal."

"I grew up with this accent." I envied her honeyed drawl. "It was worse when I first met Rue."

Life on the fringes of the Haelian Seas court as a child had left me with a crisp accent, a nasal tone, and a more rigid thought and speech pattern. I had sanded down the haughtiness until Hael brought it rushing back, snapping it in place like muscle memory.

"I set up Camp Aedan for you, in case you missed the creek, but I have a spare bedroom now."

"Rue told me about Camber. The wedding. The kids. The move to Birmingham."

About every notable moment in Arden's life too, leaving me equal parts contented and tormented.

"Hollis Apothecary Too opened last week." She rocked back on her heels. "We're officially a chain."

"Congratulations." A curve found my lips without me forcing the smile for once. "I'm glad she's happy."

"Me too." She blew out a sigh. "I miss having her as a roommate, but I visit once a month. We video chat every day and text. It's nice. Not the same, but good." She hadn't looked me in the eye once, and she didn't now. "You're wondering about your sibs." She quit fidgeting. "Rue began locating them after…" She cleared her throat. "She brought them to the farm as she found them. They've been living with Clay and Moran. They were already raising Peleg together, so what's five more daemon kids, right?"

A fist of emotion squeezed my throat. "Rue didn't tell me."

Shutting my eyes, my lashes matted with tears, I imagined Clay as the father to this brood. Chaotic, loud, and *happy* as they appeared to be, it wasn't hard to picture him raising the rough-and-tumble children as his own.

"She didn't want to say anything until we had collected the full set." Arden twisted her toe into the dirt. "We only found Caressa ten months ago. She was the last one. By that time, Rue felt it was safer not to tell you anything that might encourage you to rebel against Calixta so close to your contract ending."

By that point, I would have chewed glass at every meal and smiled as blood stained my teeth if it meant I got to walk out the doors the second my time expired. But I could see why Rue would worry. I had seen her, Asa, and Saint once a month, every month, after the ink on their bargain with the queen had dried.

Those visits saved my sanity. Maybe even my soul. Not only did they tether me to the person I had been, but they altered how Calixta treated me. I was elevated from nuisance or plaything to potential ally in an understated war she waged against Rue to convince her to take my place as heir to the Haelian throne.

Rue passed, of course, but by then it had been too late for Calixta to take back her, if not kindness, then tolerance of me. Calixta and I parted on amicable terms, and she bestowed the title on her infant son. The unexpected child had been born after a dalliance with a visiting Haelian Seas noble.

From time to time, I wondered if Saint had laced the queen's drink with a fertility spell to spare his child, but he only smiled the one time Rue hinted at the same suspicions. Perhaps he thought Calixta deserved a second chance to be a parent, the same opportunity he got with Rue. Or maybe the gods had given me a gift in ensuring my replacement, guaranteeing I could leave without further negotiation or bloodshed.

"I figured you would visit the farm first." She popped her knuckles. "Everyone is waiting for you there."

That was where Rue told me to go, but my feet led me here. "I had to come."

"She told you the kids were here," Arden guessed, nodding in understanding.

"No." I had wasted a decade, I wasn't wasting another second. "I had to see you."

Warmth spread across her cheekbones. "You're still in fascination with me."

"I am."

"You're sure?" She dragged her upper teeth over her bottom lip. "I'm not the same person I was then."

She was harder, stronger. But then again, so was I.

"Neither am I." I lifted my hand, my palm itching to cradle her cheek. "May I?"

"Yes," she breathed, leaning into my touch, closing her eyes as she anointed my fingers with her tears.

"I thought about you every day."

"I missed you." Her lashes glittered when they rose. "I tried to date, to move on, but…"

She finally, *finally* looked at me, and time ground to a halt as grief and joy shone in her eyes.

"I'm glad." I stroked her soft skin with my thumb. "I only ever wanted the best for you."

"Yeah, well, I put in the effort. I never said it was a success." She flashed her wrist again. "One of your scales, really?"

"You're more offended I marked you with a scale than me being in fascination with you?"

"There's a little thing called *consent* we need to discuss." She rolled her eyes. "But I would have said yes. I think you knew that. You wouldn't have done it otherwise. You're not a selfish person."

"You have no idea how selfish I can be when it comes to you." I clamped my jaw shut. "I shouldn't—"

"I've waited long enough to hear what you have to say to me, don't you think?"

All the things I wanted to tell her got lodged in my throat. I wasn't sure what I ought to say about my time with Calixta. If I should say anything at all. I didn't want her to think I was broken. Even if I was. I knew my family would piece me back together. No. They would help me piece *myself* back together. But that would take time. Time I wasn't willing to steal from her when I had already taken so much.

"I want you to be happy."

"Good." She took my hand and rested it on her hip. "I want that too." She hiccupped, just once, and it took me back. I saw the girl she had been in the flush heating her cheeks. "I also want this."

Rolling onto her toes, she pressed her lips to mine in a gentle kiss that gave and gave without taking.

It was a greeting. It was forgiveness. It was a promise.

Perfect.

"I want to try this." She spoke the words against my mouth. "Me and you."

Hands clutching the back of her shirt, I murmured, "I do too."

"Stop being gross out there," Daniel yelled through the screen door, a perfect mimic of Clay. "There are children present."

"There's a tub of your old clothes in the living room," Arden said, "if you want to change before we go."

The tunic and trousers I wore were the last remaining vestiges of my tenure as prince. I burned the rest. I had returned home the same as I left it—with only the clothes on my back.

"I'd like that." I kept hold of her, my grip locked on. "I seem to be having difficulty letting you go."

"Then don't." She took my hand and laced our fingers. "You can hold on for as long as you want."

"What if I want forever?"

"Then we take forever one day at a time." She squeezed my hand. "I'm not going anywhere."

"Neither am I," I promised her, daring to brush my lips across her knuckles. "Never again."

ABOUT THE AUTHOR

USA Today best-selling author Hailey Edwards writes about questionable applications of otherwise perfectly good magic, the transformative power of love, the family you choose for yourself, and blowing stuff up. Not necessarily all at once. That could get messy.

www.HaileyEdwards.net

ALSO BY HAILEY EDWARDS

Dead in the Water #1

Head Above Water #2

Hell or High Water #3

Gemini Series Novellas

Fish Out of Water

Lorimar Pack Series

Promise the Moon #1

Wolf at the Door #2

Over the Moon #3

Araneae Nation

A Heart of Ice #.5

A Hint of Frost #1

A Feast of Souls #2

A Cast of Shadows #2.5

A Time of Dying #3

A Kiss of Venom #3.5

A Breath of Winter #4

A Veil of Secrets #5

Daughters of Askara

Everlong #1

Evermine #2

Eversworn #3

Wicked Kin

Soul Weaver #1

Printed in Great Britain
by Amazon

38530600R00131